A HAUNTING TOUCH

'It was a long and gloomy night that gathered on me, haunted by the ghosts of many hopes, of many dear remembrances, many errors, many unavailing sorrows and regrets.'
– Charles Dickens, *David Copperfield*

'The act of writing requires a constant plunging back into the shadow of the past where time hovers ghost-like.'
– Ralph Ellison

A HAUNTING TOUCH

Edited by
Tinashe Mushakavanhu and A. J. Morgan

Parthian
The Old Surgery
Napier Street
Cardigan
SA43 1ED

www.parthianbooks.co.uk

First published in 2007
© The authors 2007
All Rights Reserved

ISBN: 978-1-905762-29-3

Edited by Tinashe Mushakavanhu and A. J. Morgan

Cover design and typesetting by Lucy Llewellyn
Cover photograph by Tyler Guthrie
Printed and bound by Dinefwr Press, Llandybïe, Wales

The publisher acknowledges the financial support of the Welsh
Books Council.

British Library Cataloguing in Publication Data

A cataloguing record for this book is available from the British
Library.

One need not be a chamber to be haunted,
One need not be a house;
The brain has corridors surpassing
Material place.

Ourself, behind ourself concealed,
Should startle most;
Assassin, hid in our apartment,
Be horror's least.

Emily Dickinson

CONTENTS

POETRY

Foreword

M.R. James, arguably *the* writer of ghost stories, remarked on the ambiguous attractions of fearful curiosity:

> Everyone can remember a time when he has carefully searched his curtains and poked in the dark corners of his room before retiring to rest with a sort of pleasurable uncertainty as to whether there might not be a saucer-eyed skeleton or a skinny-chested ghost in hiding somewhere.

Even, or perhaps especially, in these days of growing scepticism and materialism, and not least the power of technology to banish much, if not all actual darkness, we crave this 'pleasurable uncertainty' more than ever. It is certainly true that the contributors to *A Haunting Touch*, an anthology produced by writers, most of whom are studying on the MA Creative Writing course at Trinity College, are interested in 'pok[ing] in ... dark corners' of many kinds.

James also reminds us that the darkest of corners can be found in the most mundane of places; and this is a realisation that informs much of the work here. Davena G. Hooson, David Oakwood, A. J. Morgan and Liz Hambley all explore a sense that secrets, especially family secrets, lie in wait for all of us, in supermarkets as much us they do in the undergrowth; and that we all fear that there is, to borrow a phrase from Morgan's story, 'someone standing in the ... doorway' even as we know, or hope, that the room is empty. Yet, in another sense touched on in the poems of Naomi K. Bagel, Guinevere Clarke and Jamie White, fearing that the door connecting us to those who have died, be they old or young, may be closed to us is even more unsettling.

Death is the last taboo. A. J. Morgan explores this in a sonnet to his father reminiscent of the work of Tony Harrison; and Naomi K. Bagel hauntingly reminds us in the hugely powerful confessional piece *Leo (My lovely son who died aged six)* that words can never really touch it: there 'isn't much to say', but we feel compelled to record this very failure.

Of course, as Oakwood suggests in both his prose and poetry, this sense of failure touches us in other ways too. We can be haunted by more than ghosts; and skeletons, sometimes almost literally in the closet, take many forms: the sexual violence sanctioned by society in his biting poem *Barbie Girl* or in a different sense in other pieces by Guinevere Clark; and the more general sense, identified playfully in a story by Bagel, and more unsettlingly still in the sparse atmospheric prose of Tyler Guthrie that 'looming in the background is responsibility'.

And, if Guthrie is interested in the responsibility of the writer directly, others here seek to explore the ways in which spectres of a larger kind loom over personal stories. Diana

Beloved weaves the memories of an Italian immigrant family with the events of Aberfan; Megan Haggerty explores the similar role of Vietnam in the late Twentieth Century American psyche, a 'burden that only grows heavier with time'; and Tinashe Mushakavanhu explores in both prose and poetry, the ways in which many contemporary Zimbabweans are forced to 'imagine phantoms to keep our minds from the hunger and poverty that marked our lives'. All of these stories, like much of the best work here might be said, in the reviewer's cliché, to haunt the reader. And so they should. Whatever our tendency to dismiss the gothic and similar genres as escapist or childish, this anthology deals with what Guinevere Clark rightly calls 'no bullshit situation[s]'.

Having said that, there is much more here, too, that is inventively fanciful, echoing M.R. James' sense of the importance of pleasure: Mary Houseman writes of 'a shoe fanatic ghost' with a penchant for stilettos; and Jamie White's narrator of being given advice by the presence of Gerard Depardieu ('a big lad') which appears in the impression made in the pillow in his dishevelled and empty bed.

Finally, I should record my own sense of being watched by the past here. This anthology marks the tenth year of the MA in Creative Writing at Trinity College; and the contributors, and the stories they tell, gratifyingly echo the sentiments of the founder of the course, Jon Dressel, and the many people who have supported in it the last decade: that it should encourage a community of writers in West Wales but also have an international dimension. Dressel is rightly joined here by his successor, Menna Elfyn; and in a fittingly uncanny echo one writes of a father spinning gothic and mythic bedtime stories for a daughter, whilst the other reflects ironically on a grown poet, unable as a daughter to speak to her father, now dead. Both share with the other writers here a sense of what Elfyn calls the 'lightning-strike of story'. And, although Dressel promises the daughter of his poem 'unhaunted sleep', after reading this anthology, I cannot promise you the same.

Dr Paul Wright
Trinity College, Carmarthen

SHORT STORIES

3, Back Riley Terrace

Davena G. Hooson

I could see no further ahead of me than the length of my arm, my hand barely visible in the brown, smoke-stained fog. The air about me was cold and stank of drains, chimney fumes, wool dust and the catarrhal smell of boiled suet.

I stepped carefully across the slimy cobbles searching for the step up onto the pavement, adjusted the heavy sack on my back and tucked my chin into the warm folds of my scarf. I saw the kerb, lit by the pale yellow glimmer of a street lamp, its lantern-shape seeming to hang suspended in the smog. I stopped beneath it to read the numbers on the few envelopes I held in my hand then moved off, knowing that the numbers on the houses would be barely discernible.

The houses themselves were narrow, one up, one down; blackened, both with age and grime. They were terraced houses, each with a small front yard which contained their privies and their bin shelters. They were Victorian workers' houses and they

1

looked it – shoulder-to-shoulder, sturdy, inelegant, nothing attractive about them. These cramped streets huddled around the parent-factory walls, where many of the locals still worked.

There seemed to be no lights on in any of the houses. The occupants would be at work themselves by now as the morning shift in the factories started even earlier than mine.

Part of my round took me to Back Riley Terrace. It was very poorly lit by only one lamp, suspended under the entrance archway. Hardly any light escaped either into the court or onto the pavement before it. Entering the court I was immediately surrounded by the overpowering stench that filled much of this neighbourhood – bittersweet and foul. The maintenance of the property was non-existent – the drainpipes overflowed so that the yards were frequently covered in either pools of filthy water or thick ice. The cobbles and flagstones stuck up at angles so it was easy to miss your footing in the dark. The bottoms of each door had been gnawed away by generations of rats – the draughts inside must have been bitter.

That morning I had another letter for the occupant of number 3, Back Riley Terrace. Mrs Czerny was a woman I had never seen but who received locally posted letters at regular intervals. Her filthy doorway was running with moisture and the small, iron letterbox was too narrow for the envelope. I tried not to fold the envelope, as the contents seemed rather stiff. Could be a Christmas card. I had to bend it into a U-shape to pass it through the opening. As I turned I thought I heard the steps of someone inside the house unevenly but hurriedly descending a wooden staircase. I waited, heard nothing more so continued with my round.

Three mornings later Mrs. Czerny had another letter. Snow had fallen since my last visit and the court was filled with packed-down snow and ice where people had walked. Mrs.

Czerny's doorstep was clear. She had obviously been busy with a small coal-shovel as I could see the little soot-smeared mounds to one side of the door where she had tapped it clean. As I put the letter through the letterbox I heard the shuffle of feet on a linoleum floor. I called out,

'Post, Mrs. Czerny!'

I waited, looking at the doorstep. In the gap beneath the door I noticed a fringe of dirty, wet towelling – a make-shift solution to keeping out the draughts and snow. I turned to leave, looked up and saw a small boy with a very red nose standing under the archway lamp. I walked towards him.

'You're up and about early!' I said.

'I know,' he replied. His hands were bare and looked very raw.

'Aren't you cold, just standing about?' I asked. He looked surprised as if the thought hadn't occurred to him.

'I'm used to it, me,' he said. 'Is there owt in there for our house?' he grinned, nodding towards the sack on my shoulder.

'What's your name?'

'Wayne.'

'Well, where do you live Wayne?' I said. 'What number? What street?' He gesticulated with his thumb.

'Over thear,' he said simply. I started to walk to the next street on my round.

'That's not much help. That could be anywhere.'

'You talk posh,' he said accusingly. I stopped.

'I don't talk posh. I talk different, that's all,' I said.

'Why's that, then?' he asked.

'I used to live somewhere else,' I said. 'A place called Ludlow.'

Wayne yelled with laughter. 'Ludlow! Do they all talk posh rahnd thear?'

'Course not!' I said. He looked accusingly at me. 'I came to

3

live here about four years ago. I did go to school here.' The stare persisted. 'Anyway, I'm off now. I've to finish off this round before the middle of next week, you know!' I paused. 'You'd better go home. Your Mum and Dad'll be wondering what's happened to you.'

'They won't,' he said, positively. I took the elastic off the bundle of letters I was holding. 'You're not the usual postman. You're not even a man!'

'I'm doing it to help out over Christmas. I'm a student but my Dad works at the Post Office,' I said. I remembered Dad hadn't been all that keen on me doing this round. Said the area was a bit 'rough'. 'We get quite long holidays, students.'

'What's a student?' Wayne demanded.

'I'm studying at university,' I began.

'Don't believe ya!' he declared, and ran off.

The snow fell heavily for the next few days. Many of the outlying villages were cut off because of the drifts. Only the fit could get about, bundled up in layers of clothes.

The weather was the talk of everyone on the bus home. I sat upstairs in the smoky, blue air and popped a toffee into my mouth, looking out at the monochrome shades of snow, slush, streets, walls and pavements as the bus swayed its way through the crowded roads leaving the town centre. The driver, seeing a gap in the traffic, put his foot down and we swerved onto Wainstalls Street. An elderly woman in a maroon beret cackled with laughter as she clung onto the handle at the corner of the seat.

'Ey up! It's as good as goin' on't waltzer!' she cried. Next to her, the pale young girl wearing too much eyeliner ignored her and lit up her Embassy. A fat man in front of me spoke out of the corner of his mouth to the man next to him.

4

'D'y'ear about the bus that skidded and flattened t' top of a bus shelter?'

'Aye. It were a bad do, that,' replied the smaller man. He blew his nose and missed what the fat man said next.

'I said, it's about bloody time they sorted these roads out. It can be bottle ice up our way but all it's got to do around 'Fur-coat Green' is look a bit frosty and they're there! Grittin' fit to bust!' He sighed. 'Meks you wonder, dun't it?'

The bus stopped outside a small, corner barber's shop. Every day I noticed the painted writing on the windows – all in capitals with the Ns and Ss back to front. A young couple got off. In her thin high-heels and his Cuban heels they slid about a great deal. The bus moved off, slowly up the hill. We passed a Victorian school with a covered play-area, then a factory, the yard bustling with activity.

We moved past the stub-ends of streets where the terraced houses had gleaming windows clad in lace curtains, shining painted doors, doorsteps marked with special yellow chalk in that way that Yorkshire women like to do, and where the snow was shovelled carefully into the gutter so that each house had a clear run to the front door. Some houses had a short course of steps with matching iron railings and mud-scrapers. The colours were seldom bright. These people liked the rich, deep colours of sobriety and modesty: deep maroons; black and white; sap green; ruby. There was one door painted a bright, daffodil yellow, but the wife was French.

I lived five miles out of town, but the bus stopped a mile short, due to the snow. A small band of us set off silently for home while the bus manoeuvred its way, via a six point turn, back to the bus station.

Usually, this wide road was bordered on both sides by dry-stone walls and large fields. Now, the snowdrifts, at least six feet high, covered the fields and the walls and formed white interlocking dunes across the road. Here and there they tapered down before spilling over into the fields, so it was just possible to push through. We hurried home hiding our faces from the stinging spray of wind and snow.

Mrs. Czerny only received one Christmas card, and I'd already delivered it. The bundles of mail became a lot smaller after the Christmas rush, but I was pleased to notice Mrs. Czerny kept receiving letters. They were thin and didn't look much of a read and the address was often scrawled as if the sender was in a hurry, but they were better than nothing. It was always the same handwriting and I was able to recognise it at a glance while sorting out my mail into street bundles before I set off on my round. I was always glad to see the small envelopes addressed to her, knowing her circumstances as I did, and I began to look out for them, remembering the hurried sounds on the other side of the door whenever she heard my arrival. I crossed the court, once more covering my nose from both cold and smells and headed for the corner door. I delivered Mrs. Czerny's letter and shouted to tell her. I had kept up the practice of calling out to her, mainly, I suppose, to let her know there was someone friendly about. She had never responded and I had never seen her.

That afternoon the weather eased off a bit and I went to see a friend of mine who lived on Murcoat Green. Janet and I hadn't met for months and I was looking forward to hearing all her news. I caught the bus in the town centre, found a seat downstairs and paid my fare. I don't know what drew my attention to the woman who came to sit in front of me.

Something about her was familiar. She wore an old, but thick coat and a black headscarf, heavily patterned with roses. A familiar whiff of Back Riley Terrace tickled the back of my throat.

The conductor came to take her fare and I listened with interest. The woman gave him a coin then held up both hands, fingers spread. Then she closed them into fists and then held all fingers out again.

'You want a twenty pence ticket, love?' the conductor yelled. The woman nodded and took the ticket.

I was able to watch unobserved as she began to burrow in the brown, plastic shopping bag on her lap. She drew out an envelope and took out the paper inside. I recognised the envelope and the writing on it. I *was* sitting behind Mrs. Czerny. I turned to see where the conductor was but he had gone to collect the upstairs fares. I stretched my neck and managed to see the contents of the letter.

I knew the handwriting as well as I knew my own. The language was foreign to me and began with the single word, 'Mamo'. It looked as if it could have been Polish – or something like it. The end of the letter was signed 'Irene'.

The single sheet of paper trembled and more than once I noticed her wipe her cheeks with her fingers. I swallowed hard.

I decided to follow her.

The wind was bitter as I reached the corner. I had followed her for several minutes and she had obviously made this journey many times. She approached the tall gates of a large house. I had visited this house before Christmas when I had been on the parcel round. That was a cushy job if your deliveries were mostly in the town. They give you a van and you can stop for a bit if you time it right. Suddenly I stopped. Mrs. Czerny was on her knees in the gateway.

I thought she'd had an attack of some sort and I was about to rush over when I saw her cross herself then kiss a long string of beads around her neck. I stood there, watching her kneeling in slush and ice, listening to her quiet moans. I wanted to go and help her but I felt she would resent any interference. I had no idea what to do.

I anxiously watched as she crossed herself once more, wiped her eyes and cheeks with a large handkerchief then pulled herself to her feet using the bars of the gate to help. I darted back around the corner and waited until she had gone. I was so distressed by what I had seen that I had to wait a few minutes before I continued the walk to Janet's.

'So, do you know who lives there? I know I've delivered there, but I can't remember.' I had told Janet that the large house with the barred gates I'd passed on the way had impressed me. I told her nothing about the tragic figure I had watched at those gates.

'Yes. Do you remember Sandra?'

'Sandra Greenwood?'

'Yes. Well her Mum used to clean for the people who live there. He owns a mill and it's done very well. Makes covers for car seats and whatnot.'

'Hargreaves Mill?' I said.

'That's him. Him and his wife live there. Have done for years.'

'No children?' I asked.

'Yes. Three, I think. Packed off to boarding school, though. So you can tell what sort of people they are.' She bit into her slice of Victoria sponge. 'I can't understand folk who get rid of their children like that. It's as if they're saying, "There, I've had the things, we've done our duty and given the family some heirs, but I don't want the responsibility of bringing them up." Isn't it?'

I agreed.

'They're moving, anyway, so it'll be up for sale soon. Interested?' She laughed and took another bite of her cake.

'Hello, Sandra?' I asked.

'Yes, speaking.' I recognised her voice immediately. When I told her who was calling she seemed very pleased. We exchanged news and joked for several minutes, but inevitably, soon began to run out of things to say to each other.

'Anyway, the thing is, I understand your mum used to know a family who live on Crossley Lane. Do you remember them?'

'Yes! Of course I do. I used to go there sometimes and play with one of the kids. Dead posh, but they were okay.'

'Did you ever hear if they had any relatives living close by?'

'We're talking about the Hargreaves family aren't we?'

'Yes, they own the factory.'

'Right.' There was a pause. 'I don't think he'd got anyone to speak of. I do have a feeling that there was a Mum somewhere in the picture. Hers, I think. Lived in Poland.'

'So, the wife's Polish?'

'Mrs. Hargreaves? Yes, but no accent whatsoever. You'd never know. Talks with a mouth full of plums. Hell of a snob! She's called, er... No. I've forgotten. But she's the one who rules the roost.'

'Was her name Irene?' I asked.

'Oh, yes. It was. Irene.' There was a pause and I could hear her tapping her teeth with a pencil. 'I remember my mum telling me once that the children had to wear aprons when eating their meals, even the boys, and weren't allowed to leave the table until they had each recited a psalm!'

'You're joking! A psalm?'

'I'm not! Yeah! A psalm!'

'What, every meal?'

'No, every evening meal. Before they could go and watch TV or anything, they had to do this psalm.' She sighed. 'Cold bitch.'

'That was the mum's idea, then?'

'Oh yes. Mrs. Hargreaves was a stickler for rules and regulations. And this went on even when they were at university or in the sixth form. Not just little kids!'

'And what about the grandma. The one in Poland?' I asked. 'I don't know anything about her. As far as Mrs. Hargreaves was concerned, I think she felt that that was all in the past.'

'So you never saw her?'

'Well, no – she lived in Poland!'

'Right.'

I changed the subject and we talked for a little while longer until the conversation petered out. I was on the point of saying goodbye when Sandra suddenly interrupted.

'They're off to America, did you know?' she said. I immediately knew she meant the Hargreaves family.

'I knew they were moving. But I didn't know they were leaving the country,' I replied.

'Why do you want to know about them, anyway?' she asked.

'I think I may know a relative of theirs.'

'Really? Who?'

'Oh, I'm not sure, yet, but I'll keep you posted.' I replaced the receiver and went out for a walk.

Number 3, Back Riley Terrace looked bleak and cold as usual. As I pushed the letter through the door I called out and waited. I heard the letter being opened. Almost immediately I heard a stifled sob.

I gently knocked on the door and said,

'Mrs. Czerny! I am a friend. Please let me help.' I waited, but didn't expect a reply. I got none.

'I know about Irene, Mrs. Czerny. I know about your daughter.' I paused. 'I'd like to help you, Mrs. Czerny. Please open the door.'

I waited for a good ten minutes at her door before making a move to leave, and then I noticed a slight movement of her curtain. I waved and smiled, nodded and waved trying to let her see I was harmless and friendly but it all came to nothing. Standing underneath the archway was Wayne, one of his cheeks bulging with sweets.

'What are you eating then, Wayne?' I asked.

'Gobstopper,' he said, and took it out to grin, then popped it back in. He frowned at me then took it out again to speak.

'What's up?'

'I'm a bit worried about old Mrs. Czerny at number three. She's had some bad news and she's got no-one to talk to.'

'She has,' said Wayne. 'She talks to herself.' He laughed and licked the gobstopper. 'Anyway, she's mad,' he said flippantly.

'Of course she's not mad!' I said angrily. 'She's old and alone.'

Wayne looked at me silently, smiling.

'She's very lonely,' I said, and blew my nose.

'I knew you were cryin' as soon as I saw yer!' he jeered.

I set off on the rest of my round.

11

None of my notes to the Hargreaves were answered. None of the information I sent them was acted upon, as far as I could tell. I told John, the postman whose round included Back Riley Terrace, what I knew and he said he'd 'look out' for her. My father said we couldn't interfere as the old woman had a family and it was nothing to do with us. I returned to York for the new term.

I'd been back at university for about two weeks when my parents sent me the cutting. It said that the men who went to collect the skip from the back of the empty Hargreaves house had discovered Mrs. Czerny's frozen body kneeling on the ice nearby. She must have slipped and not been able to get up. It had been a particularly cold and bitter January, it said.

The Jazz Cellar

Tyler Guthrie

Oliver is in tonight. Most assumed he would be; it's a jazz night. This assumption was confirmed for Lisa by the umbrella hanging on the chair. This umbrella was nice – expensive and old. It hung on the backrest of the far chair at table seven. The chair to Oliver's right.

Lisa would be Oliver's waitress for the evening. She knew him well, at least she knew what to expect. She saw the umbrella. He's probably in the restroom – washing his hands before everyone arrives.

Oliver was an easy table. Easy to serve, easy to check, easy to clean. Every night he's in, it's the same isn't it? The umbrella is on the chair, Oliver is nowhere to be seen. His table is arranged with the flower and the candle at the top left corner. The menu is standing at the top right – facing inwards. The napkin is folded into a triangle in the exact centre of the table pointing towards the stage. Not like the others. This is Oliver's table. I give him five minutes.

When he comes back, he will have an Espresso Cubano. He will even look at the menu.

Lisa had been working at the Cellar for three months now. Oliver was her first customer. She liked her job, she liked the Cellar. She liked Oliver – he's an easy table. He writes in the little notepad he keeps in his pocket. A yellow unimpressive thing. He covers it when people are near. Lisa peeks. He always writes about the Cellar and the people around him. He even wrote about himself once, although I'm not quite sure. He did order an Espresso Cubano though.

Many people like this place. Something about it draws them in. The walls are brick and the floors are hardwood. The ceilings are high, but most of the shop is below ground. In the morning the sunlight pours through the windows near the ceiling. Heaven sent. By the afternoon all light is artificial. The Cellar officially opens at four and closes 'late'. Those who know come for coffee and pastries in the morning, before alcohol is served and the light over the sign is illuminated. It's a place for all types, though inside it's mostly students and old men.

Lisa has about five minutes before the Cellar goes quiet. Rounds must be done, customers dealt with. I think there's enough wine on the floor for the night.

Local art adorns the walls. Many struggling artists make their first sale here. One painting in particular hangs next to the bar. It's been here since the '80s. When she first saw it, Lisa loved it. Across the bottom it says *It's Done When All is Said – If You Don't Speak, it's Not Done*. After a month she couldn't look at it anymore. Now she hates it.

Oliver should be getting back to his table soon, or he'll miss the show. The lights have already started to drop. Last orders on the espresso machine are taken.

At the Cellar, when the lights drop, jazz will shortly follow. Not *litejazz*, the shit played in elevators enjoyed by people never oppressed or at least by those who don't know what it is to feel angst in an absurd world. It's the jazz of Monk and Hampton. It's impressionism and improvisation. Music without pretence played by musicians without money. It's not performed, it's played and it's played because it's an impulse. If it weren't jazz, if it weren't music, it would be something else.

When the lights drop, the espresso machine will stop, the bar will open. The music will play – shortly at first, then build with speed, complexity, and passion. Different bands come through nightly, rarely the same. The music will dance, sweat will build. Songs fade into free jazz, solos and jams. The bass and drums also solo. Lisa will glide across the Cellar tending to her tables. Oliver will sip his Espresso Cubano slowly, meticulously. He savours it.

With the music, the club grows full, new faces and old. Jazz will seep out into the street. Past dark rows of books, floured counters, and empty chairs. It will make its way tenderly to the old estates, barely noticed until the door to the Cellar opens and melodic chaos breaks out momentarily. Then the door will close and all will be normal.

Oliver will wait in silence for the set. Before picking up his Espresso Cubano to sip, his lips will slowly part to the jazz the way the lonely do when seeing others kiss.

When the first set ends, Oliver sits. Others laugh and joke and Oliver sits. The room pulses with energy and so does Oliver – but he will continue to sit.

When the bar gets busy with new orders before the next set, Oliver will have left as others take their seat. Lisa will be busy, bringing second, third, and fourth rounds to those locked in the Cellar. She will peek over at Oliver's table, just to make sure this time he won't stay around.

By then, Oliver will be out the door. He will walk down the street past the bookstore and the bakery. Up the hill away from the Cellar. Quietly he will pass the old estates under the imposing trees that block the light from the streetlamps. He will walk slowly, carefully. He will resist the urge to step in any other way. He will stop next to the mailbox, breathe deeply and listen for the jazz. When he hears it he will smile.

He must. Lisa knows this. It's a jazz night.

Shoes

Mary Houseman

Polly was looking for her shoes. The black patent pair would go just nicely with that shiny new skirt. I'd noticed she was particular about such things. There was a lot of noise coming from the cupboard under the stairs and she came out with an angry look on her face. Then she tried a few more places, the spare room where she kept pairs in boxes, under the bed, behind the furniture. Then she gave up, found some old slip-ons that would have to do and slammed out of the house.

Imagine her surprise when she found the missing shoes on the back doorstep next morning. She turned them over as she picked them up and I do believe she sniffed them, as if they'd been returned by some wild beast. She stood looking out over the garden for a while, her fingers dabbing at the bubbles of moisture gathered on the patent. She must have been wondering if she'd left them there by mistake. But how had she missed them coming in last night? A mystery indeed! I'm sure if there'd been someone else in the house she'd have remarked on just how strange it all was. For the time being Polly put the shoes with others in a tidy row under the stairs.

Next day, and the day after that, she seemed compelled to check her shoes under the stairs. First of all, the sandals looked as though they had shifted. Then she wondered if her trainers shouldn't be there. And surely those sling-backs had been at the end of the row? And the wellies were turned round.

'You must stop imagining things,' Polly told herself. 'You haven't moved in long. You're under pressure.'

A few days later Polly went out after dark. A vehicle came to collect her. She had on a long emerald dress under which peeped the softest and palest of green shoes, pointed and with the sharpest of heels. Tripping in some hours later, in the back hall she cast off in an unusually casual fashion her leafy stilettos and fumbled her way to bed. The pale green shoes were not in the back hall next morning. Polly searched the house, even looked on the back doorstep. Just in case, she went out into the street. Well, she probably had trouble remembering anything much about last night.

I imagine she had those pretty stilettos on her mind during the day. When she came home she'd bought a new pair of shoes. These were tan leather, with a big buckle and a squared-off toe. Polly spent some time trying them on in front of her long mirror, turning her ankles, putting her feet together, pacing about. She seemed very pleased with them. Then the phone went. She tucked her new purchases beneath the dressing table and hurried downstairs.

'Oh, Fanny. Hi! Haven't heard from you for ages. You coming over soon? Tomorrow! Soon as that? Fine. You know how to find me?'

18

Polly spent the evening tidying up. Of course she knew it was only her sister but as was her habit the place must be impeccable for visitors. And this was the first time Fanny had been to the Old Mill. She announced to the silent sitting room that she would hoover first thing in the morning. It was dark by the time she was able to relax. A glass of Merlot in her hand she stepped out of the conservatory into the garden. A crisp crescent moon penetrated the birches, spreading a pale, speckled bloom on the lawn. As she wandered through her blue mules were leaving a velvet trail on the grass among the borders and shrubs. She was smiling in the peace. Just the faintest rustling of leaves. She sipped her wine. The moon dipped and reappeared on the glinting edge of a cloud. Polly glanced up and saw her leafy stilettos dangling in the branches of a birch.

'My God!' She grabbed them and dashed inside.

'What the hell!'

Polly emptied the bottle before going to bed that night but not before she'd made a point of examining closely the green stilettos and carefully settling them into a shoe box which she locked away in the wardrobe in the spare room.

Fanny seemed very impressed with her sister's new home. She wandered through every room, commenting on the old beams and the exposed stonework, the huge fireplace. She did stumble on the narrow twisting stairs but said it was worth the effort if only to get the view of the river.

'Must be a few hundred years old this place. Won't ask you if you find it spooky. Things like that never did bother you, eh?'

They were standing by the kitchen window. The birch tree just outside was trembling quite violently in the wind. Polly looked as if she was going to reveal something but she just shrugged.

'What's the town like? Any good shops?'

'Great shoe shop. Bought a pair yesterday. I'll show you.'

Polly escaped upstairs remembering she'd left the tan shoes with the buckles under the dressing table. They weren't there. Polly shuddered.

'Must have put them somewhere safe. Can't remember just now,' she confessed to her sister. 'Let's have some tea.'

When Fanny had gone, Polly sighed and slumped in an armchair. These shoes. What was she to think? Were they really disappearing? Or was her mind playing tricks? No. She hadn't imagined them dangling in the tree. After tea she decided to lock all her shoes in the wardrobe in the spare room. Every single pair!

It was getting dark when someone knocked on the front door. She stood in the hall for a while. Must have been wondering what to do. The knocking went on. There was a shuffling about out there. She'd never answered the door before. Everyone went round the back. She drew the bolts and opened up, just a crack.

'Polly! Heavens above, let me in.'

'Why didn't you come round the back?'

'It's locked and you wouldn't answer. I was banging on it for ages!' Fanny struggled in.

'What's happened? Why are you back?'

'Puncture. Not far from that garage on the main road as it happens. They'll fix it in the morning. Kind man drove me back here. Always carry a sponge bag. Lend me a nightie, eh? Put this bag in the spare room?'

Fanny was instantly up the stairs and staring at the heap of shoes and shoe boxes on the spare bed.

'What are you up to, Poll? Not throwing all these out?'

'Sorting them. That's all.'

'Never seen so many shoes.'

'Don't exaggerate. We'll just put them on the floor for now.'

Fanny began throwing them on the floor. Polly didn't seem very happy about piling them up under the window. No doubt being a tidy person she'd have preferred to put them in neat pairs.

'You seem jittery tonight. What's wrong, Poll?'

'Wasn't expecting anyone at the door. Not at night anyway. Let's get to bed. We can talk in the morning.'

For a few hours the house was quiet. The sisters slept in adjacent rooms, watched through the landing window by a plump moon. Whatever was on her mind Polly never had any trouble getting to sleep. She was in a land of crinolined ladies strutting in chandeliered halls, their buckled high heels clattering the boards, when Fanny came rushing in.

'Somebody's been in my room! Someone's shuffling about.'

'I didn't hear anything. Everything's locked up.'

'Not you, then? Wasn't you?'

'Course not!'

'Got a stick or something?'

'Fanny! Just put the light on and we'll go see.'

Polly strode in her short nightie into the spare room, switching on more lights as she went. The heap of boxes and shoes was now strewn all round the bed.

'Now, I didn't do that!'

'They must have slipped. And you caught your foot in them when you got up.'

'Polly, this place is haunted.'

'What, by a shoe fanatic ghost?'

'You've had trouble before, haven't you? Tell me!'

'Not trouble as such.' Polly was stumbling about, busy putting the shoes back. She didn't seem keen to talk.

'Don't you think we should check downstairs? Come on. Then let's have some tea. And you can tell me what's been

21

going on in this haunted house.'

Of course, there was no sign of anyone trying to break in. All was tranquillity as they supped their tea at the kitchen table.

'You're not sorry you came here then?'

'Why should I be? I like it. It's… interesting.'

'You're going to have to tell me, Poll.'

'Okay. But honestly, it's nothing much.'

So they sat there in the middle of the night and Polly told her sister about her shoes going missing. And how they came back, at least most of the time. When she got round to the leafy green shoes dangling in the tree Fanny was amazed.

'What fun! Spooky though.'

'I was wondering if someone's still got a key. A friend of the previous owner perhaps.'

'And they creep in at night to try on your shoes? Bit kinky.'

'But surely I'd hear them.'

'You'll just have to stay up. Keep a watch through the night.'

I don't suppose that thought was very appealing as they went back to bed to steal a few more hours sleep. Even so, in the morning Fanny was convinced it was a good idea. 'You do that then, Poll. Stay up and watch. And I've got another idea.'

Polly looked tired and anxious, not her usual self. Perhaps she wasn't keen on her big sister taking over.

'You ever checked out this house in the local Records Office? No? Well, I'll be round there tomorrow. Old place like this, they could very likely have something on it.'

Polly drove Fanny back to the garage to pick up her car. When she came in, she was sighing. She went up to the spare room. No point in stripping the bed. For all she knew her sister would return tomorrow, armed with goodness knows what news. She surveyed the heap of shoes under the window

22

and sorted from it a pair of walking boots, pristine clean, and shutting the door firmly, shoved on a jacket and marched off down towards the river.

It was a squally sort of day and when she returned to the house an hour or so later she looked as if she'd had a battle out there. And she wasn't alone. An old fellow followed her into the kitchen. They'd both removed their boots.

'Cup of tea, Mr Thomas?'

'Thank you, but indeed no. Just wanted to see how that old beam's holding up. Cheeky of me, I know, but when you've done a job you like to see it's right.' He put his hand on the wide piece of oak above the stove. 'Glad you never saw this place before we did it up. You'd have never come here. Animals, that's what they had in here. The cows wandering in and out as they pleased.'

'Proper working mill at one time, though?'

'Oh yes.' Mr Thomas pulled off his cap and thought for a moment. 'My Nan's... cousin. That's it. Miller. Lived here all his life, man and boy. He had some tales to tell about this place. Tales you'd never believe. Well, my dear, mustn't keep you talking. That weather looks as if it's coming on bad again.'

'Perhaps you'd come up for tea one afternoon. I'd love to hear your tales about the place.'

'Sure.' The old man patted Polly's hand. 'Not all of them are nice, my dear. Downright horrible some of them. But you just let me know and I'll pick out the best for you.'

Much of the rest of the day Polly spent wandering around, looking at parts of the house, fingering the walls, looking across beams and up chimneys. Perhaps she was after some secret cupboard, some dark hole where shoes might be hidden away. There was a set of drawings of mill workings up on the landing, big cogs and huge grinding stones and shafts where you could have a nasty accident. That's probably what she was thinking of. Finally she found her way into the spare room and set to, sorting and boxing her shoes and stacking them ever so tidy in the bottom of the wardrobe.

'There you are, shoe ghost. You try getting at them.' She looked really pleased with herself. She wasn't so pleased in the morning when she found her walking boots had gone from the back hall. When the phone went that evening Polly was very impatient.

'No I didn't stay up all night. Much too tired. And another pair's gone. My walking boots caked in mud. Can you believe it? Who on earth would want them? Anyway, did you get to the Records Office?' Fanny must have a lot to tell her.

'Did you do copies? Okay. Bring the stuff over? Oh, and by the way, I've spoken to this old bloke who lives down the road. Says he knows some horrible stories about this place.... No, it doesn't worry me!'

That night Polly dreamed her bedroom was full of dust and scattered corn and huge wooden beams and great cogs turning above her head. Her bed was the millstone and it was grinding round and round. She woke up in the moonlight, calling out. And a person was standing over her.

'What are you doing?'

'Just borrowing your slippers,' I explained.

Polly shouted as I picked them up off the floor. 'You! Just leave them.' She jumped out of bed. I thought she was going to hit me. I went out on the landing. Polly came after me.

'Give me those slippers and show me how you got in!'

I wasn't about to hand over those slippers. I drifted down the stairs.

'Suppose you pinched all the other shoes?' Polly stood on the landing.

24

'I never pinched anything! I just borrowed them. Had them all back, haven't you?' I whispered and she heard me.

'Just who are you? You've got a key, haven't you?'

'I don't need keys. And locking them won't stop me!' Then I left the house for a while. Gave Polly a chance to cool down while I tried on the slippers. She'd be on the phone to that sister of hers soon enough. I wondered what they'd make of it all!

Indeed, Fanny was over pretty quick the next day.

'You phoned the police yet, Poll?' Polly shook her head. Didn't seem able to get her words out.

'Tell me, then. What was she like, this girl?'

'Teenager. About thirteen? Smallish and very thin, long brown hair. Didn't look too healthy, but it was moonlight. What amazed me was the way she just vanished. I searched everywhere. I'm wondering if there's a secret cupboard or a way in that I don't know about.'

'Tell me, did she look like a ghost?'

'Goodness! What do ghosts look like?'

'It's just that.... Well... it might tie in with what I got from the Archives. I found an old newspaper article about a girl who worked as a servant here, in this mill. About the 1870s. She was had up for stealing from the miller's wife and this was the report of the court case. Guess what she stole Poll!'

'Oh no.'

'Yep. It's a pretty awful story. Her name was Sarah Morwent. She was sentenced to transportation. Australia, I think.'

'Doesn't sound like your ghost then.'

'Well, I found more in the paper, some months later. Sarah had somehow managed to escape from one of those hulks, you know, prison ships moored off the coast, just before she was due to be transported. The paper said she'd probably come back here.

'Good for her.'

'Pity we can't ask her.'

'Ask what?'

'If it's her, of course.'

'Of course it's not her! This isn't a ghost, Fanny. It must be some girl who's heard the story, from that old fellow probably, and she's out for a bit of fun.'

'Well, I think it's Sarah and she's always had a fancy for shoes.'

'I'll ask the old fellow, Mr Thomas.'

When Fanny had gone home I thought it was time to put Polly's boots back in the hall. I had quite taken to them after I'd cleaned them up. They were much like a pair I'd had as a small child but made of a finer leather, though the soles weren't so thick. I must admit I was tempted to hold on to them, but I'd promised myself I'd always give them back.

Of course Polly was amazed to see them in the morning clean and shining, almost new. I do believe I saw her smile. Perhaps she was getting used to me being about. I was waiting to see what she would find out from Mr Thomas. Just a day or so later he was knocking at Polly's door.

'Sarah Morwent? Oh yes. That's quite a tale, that is. Drowned in the river out there. Well, that's what they say.'

'Drowned!'

'They say people round here were proud of her escaping off that prison ship. Not so miller's wife. She wanted her took back. Reported her to the constable. Said she'd seen her walking after dark along the riverbank, just opposite here. True or not, I don't know.'

'Not a nice person, that miller's wife.'

'They say not. Anyway, she didn't get her way, did she?

Poor old Sarah went into the river. She wasn't going back to that prison, or Australia for that matter.'

'That's so sad. Never seen again?'

'They do say.'

Poor Polly had a restless night after that. In fact she stayed awake watching for me. I drifted up the stairs and into her room about midnight. I stood in the doorway, in the pale lunar light. Polly was sitting on the side of her bed.

'Have you brought my slippers?'

'Oh dear, I forgot them.'

'Tell me, Sarah Morwent, why do you steal my shoes?'

'I like shoes. After all this time I've found some what fit.'

'What a cheek!'

'I always bring them back, Polly. I don't steal them.'

'The miller's wife didn't think so.'

'She had mostly clogs and boots. She wasn't pleased that I borrowed her one good pair of shoes.'

'She reported you and you went to prison!'

'Indeed! But for that I paid her back.'

'What do you mean?'

'Pushed her in the river, the bitch!'

'The Miller's wife drowned?... I thought...'

'Aye. You thought it was me went in the river. I hear people saying that all the time.'

Polly stood up. She looked scared.

'Couldn't have been me,' I assured her, laughing. 'I'm still here, see? Still borrowing shoes.'

Bloody Mary

David Oakwood

She, like me, was staring at the Ready Meals for One. From behind she looked like my grandmother. Wispy white hair around her shoulders, a slightly crooked back, wearing a thick grey coat and front-seamed, flared beige trousers. *Will I wear dull colours when I am old?* I'd thought, before looking into the refrigerator cabinet and asking myself if I could still be a vegetarian if I indulged, just this once, in the enticing comfort of the sausage hotpot?

She looked up from the shepherd's pie and stared straight into my eyes. Jesus! I'd never seen anything like it. She had bright red lipstick on her lopsided smile, it emphasised the stroke tilt to her mouth by having been painted on at an angle, missing her narrow lips as though a child had done it. Her eyes were deep set and grey-blue, they struck me at once as wild and distant, hidden beneath the cornice of her boney eye sockets. Her whole face was painted with snow white slap, which gathered in the furrows of her brow. Her eyebrows had been plucked to nothing, and the snow had settled in the chicken skin pits.

I struggled to smile back, my mouth intent on remaining in an open gape of shock. She was pantomimic. Like Queen Elizabeth the First on whom all drag queens model their make-up. I wondered briefly in that instant if she was indeed a man in drag. She was certainly a queen saying, 'One never knows what to fancy.'

'Yeah.'

I could have turned away at that point, the brief exchange, possible in a supermarket or dentist's waiting room, was all the social etiquette required. But the voyeur in me found her fascinating.

'I can't decide if I'm a vegetarian.'

'Don't do it. You need the blood of others or you'll fade away. That's why vegans are so thin. They're slowly disappearing.'

It was then I noticed her long fingers caressing the wrapping of a venison slab in the basket of her small shopping trolley. I surveyed the other contents and found that she had bacon rashers, Lincolnshire sausages and a steak and kidney pie. The only contents that had not at some point taken their first steps were the cartons of tomato juice, the bottle of Tesco's value vodka and the Worcester sauce.

She smiled up at me then and her false teeth slipped from their gums revealing two jagged broken canines. She sucked her dentures back up and I averted my eyes to stare back down at her purchases. She said, 'I shall, of course, buy some fruit.'

I laughed. What else could I do? Words evaded me. At this point I glanced down at my own trolley containing copies of *Hello* and *Heat* magazines headlined with 'Celebrity Make-Up Disasters'. I rather cruelly wished I could photograph the old woman and submit the photo for £100. But she wasn't famous. Cradled in the basket at the end of my trolley was a bunch of flowers, for my grandmother's grave.

'Someone special?' she asked, picking up two shepherd's pies and flicking her eyes towards the yellow chrysanthemums.

'Oh, no, well yes, they're my grandmother's favourites.'

'Lovely.'

'For her grave. It's been a year.'

'Sad. That she died.'

'She was eighty-four. Batty as a fruitcake and longing to go really.'

'No one wants to die.'

This annoyed me, re-kindling a sense of guilt I'd battled with.

'Gran did. She said it's time she left and let me find the time to let a man into my life. She started hiding her pills.'

I must be as lonely as she looks, I'd thought, why the hell was I telling her this? She began to caress the venison again saying, 'When my sister Annabella died she went screaming.'

Hairs stood on end down the back of my neck, the refrigerator cabinets became suddenly colder.

'Oh... sorry... Annabella... beautiful name,' I was mumbling.

'They lumped me with Mary.'

I couldn't speak, the talking trailed off unnaturally. I began to side away, crossed the aisle and pretended briefly to look at the baked beans before walking off towards the checkouts.

As the teenage boy struggled to make the flowers scan I told myself that I was being stupid. Thousands of women were called Mary. I grabbed the bouquet and scanned it myself.

I was knelt down, struggling to arrange the chrysanthemums in

Gran's urn as a cold wind whipped about me. I looked up as I felt the presence of someone beside me. She was bending over me; waving slowly, her teeth in a fixed grin. I jumped out of my skin and to my feet. My hand shot instinctively towards my throat.

'Annabella is buried here,' and she turned around revealing a white marble stone facing my grandmother's grave which read '*Annabella O'Dwyer, Beloved Daughter, born 2.4.1947 died 2.4.1951. Always Remembered*'.

'I was seven. Annabella was four. She drowned in the bath on her birthday.'

'Oh God.'

'It wasn't God. She got the kitten I had wanted. I lost my temper in the bath.'

My family name is O'Dwyer. Knots tightened in my stomach. I could taste sick bubbling at the base of my throat.

'They thought Annabella was an angel. She was such a good girl. He used to beat me. Daddy hated me. They sent me to St Christopher's to stop my Daddy killing me. I stayed there for forty-two years.'

There was an uncomfortable pause.

'I... don't understand. Why are you following me?'

She smiled and she reached for my hand but I was already walking away, backwards at first but then turning at quite a pace, almost tripping myself as I started to run. My mother's name was Mary. She had run away aged fifteen having abandoned me on my grandmother's door step with a note saying 'Please'. Or that's what I'd been told anyway. Gran didn't know who my father was. The vampire drag queen was my mother.

She knocked on my door two days later. I let her in.

Memorial Days

Megan Haggerty

I was home alone the day I learned my brother was killed. The majority of the day was like any other, but the news I learned that afternoon left a deep scar on my world forever. The memory of what happened still is and always will be as crushing as when I lived it. In fact, I re-live it even to this day. Indiscriminate as to when it all flashes back to me, I find myself distant from the task at hand while I remember arriving home from school on that April afternoon.

It was usual for no one to be there to greet me. I was eleven years old and in the sixth grade and my mom worked evenings at JC Penny. Since my grandmother lived in our apartment building, one floor below, Mom figured I'd be all right on my own for a few hours each night. I wasn't allowed to answer the door or tell anyone on the phone that I was home by myself, so I just locked myself inside and ignored any calls.

On this particular day, I came in with a growling stomach.

Tossing my school bag aside, I made a bee-line for the kitchen. My insufficient lunch consisted of a few crackers, some slices of cheese, a soft apple that had passed being ripe and fifteen cents to buy a carton of milk from the lunch lady. Running late, I had packed it in a rush that morning. I picked at it during lunchtime, but ended up throwing the apple and most of the dry crackers away. Now at home, I searched the cabinets and found an almost empty jar of peanut butter and an unopened loaf of bread. I used a knife to scrape the bottom of the jar and licked the stray peanut butter off my fingers. Leaving the mess, I brought my sandwich to the living room and flipped on the television.

Just as I sank my teeth into the soft bread, there was a knock on the door. It was a loud, solid KNOCK. KNOCK. KNOCK. I didn't move right away. There was something different about this knock but I couldn't place my finger on it. An unsettling feeling inside me urged me to find out who was at the door. Waiting a few moments longer, I opened the door wide enough to watch the visitors leave. My stomach immediately sank to the floor and my heart thumped at a faster and harder pace. *Marines.* They were Marines. Swinging the door open, I went after them.

'Is this about my brother?'

They turned and looked at me. There were three of them, three men all tall and powerful dressed in dark, proud uniforms. They said nothing as I approached them, and only loomed over me with expressionless faceless.

'Are you here about my brother?' I asked again, the words straining to get out of my throat.

Finally, after what felt like hours of hesitation, one responded, 'We need to talk to your mother. Is she home?'

'No, she's at work.'

33

He looked down at a sheet of paper. 'JC Penny?'

'Yes.'

'Thank you. Go back inside, okay?'

'But what about my brother?'

This time they ignored me and went down the stairs. I followed them down to the next floor and while they continued, I ran through the hall to my grandmother's apartment. I banged my fists against the door until she answered. By this time the tears poured like flood water down my cheeks. I couldn't speak.

'Marines,' was all that came out. I pointed to the stairs.

Without a word, my grandmother responded to my directions. I tightly grasped the handrail as we rushed down the stairs. It saved me as I tripped repeatedly in my desperate attempt to reach the Marines before they left. Out in the blinding sun, I scanned the parked cars and a black Cadillac caught my attention. The men had just sat inside and were about to close their doors. We ran towards the car, waving our arms. A few words were exchanged, but all of them having nothing to do with the purpose of their visit. We all knew why they were there. It was Johnny. My brother was dead.

They told my mother I was sick to get her to come home from work. My grandmother called her and hid the pain in her voice the best she could. Back inside the apartment, we sat with the soldiers in silence while we waited for her to come home. During that time, thoughts sped through my mind, faster than I could process them. *How did it happen? I didn't want to know. Maybe this was a mistake, and they thought we were someone else's family. How could I not see my brother again? This isn't happening.*

The quiet was broken by the sound of keys in the door. Our eyes shot over to watch my mom enter the room. I studied her face as it went pale when she saw the Marines and the realization of what it all meant slapped her. Her knees went weak and the men rushed to help her to a seat. Loud, choking sobs followed while my grandmother tried to comfort her.

I didn't know what to do. *Should I go over to her? Say something to her? Should I keep out of the way?* I felt helpless. So I just stayed where I was observing the scene as it unfolded before me. I watched until eventually my own eyes welled up with tears and I couldn't see anymore.

No matter where I am, remembering that scene, my eyes continue to well up with tears. When I'm alone I allow myself to cry in an attempt to release the burden that only grows heavier with time. It's more painful when I can't have those moments. I have to keep it hidden while I'm at work, in the grocery store, or if I'm in a conversation. This kind of pain is too personal, too unfamiliar to those who haven't experienced it.

'It's been almost forty years,' they say. 'Why aren't you over it?'

I never respond. The kind of people who would ask that question aren't the kind of people who could comprehend the honest answer. Of course I would never wish this kind of suffering on anyone, so let them ask their ignorant questions. The best I can attempt to do is share what kind of person he was so that they might have a glimpse of what he represented in my life.

Johnny was the glue that held my family together. With my parents' divorce and my sister Rita married and starting her own family, he was the constant force I could rely on. To all of us he was already a hero, and joining the Marines just put him in a uniform. He was only nineteen when he was sent to Vietnam but even from there he continued to unify us. He wrote letters, making jokes and pouring out affection in words that were far beyond his years. We should have been the ones encouraging him while he was on the battlefield and yet he was the one who kept us going. Of course he spared the women in the family the horrible truths of war. He never mentioned having to witness the deaths of his friends or having to kill enemy soldiers. Those were the painful stories he shared only with my father. With everything he was experiencing he was still thinking of us before himself. He was always doing that, protecting me.

There were certain situations in my life that were made more bearable because of Johnny. My mother's drinking was one of them. When my thoughts drift further back in time, before his death, I remember the times during his life where he stepped in and took the worry and the fear away, if only for a few hours. One time in particular stands out above the rest. Johnny had shut the family room door, where our mother sat, passed out in front of the TV. I watched as he grabbed his jacket from the closet and slipped his arms into the sleeves. The panic of being left home alone with my mother sank down in my stomach. But before Johnny shut the closet door, he took my jacket off the hanger.

'C'mon Karen,' he said as he helped me put on my coat. 'We're going out.'

'But what about your date?'

'You are my date. The best date I could ever have. Let's go.'

He gripped my hand and held the front door open for me. My hand stung a little from his strong grasp, but I didn't mind. More than pain, I felt safe and vulnerable. It was a comfortable vulnerability. The kind where you don't mind because you know you're protected. It's the way all children should feel. When I was with my brother, he helped me to forget all the bad stuff and just be a kid.

Life after he died provided the worst of feelings and experiences I ever had to go through. Things became increasingly unstable and miserable. Worse than the external conditions that were hurting me were the emotions and insecurities brewing inside me. He was still continuing to affect me and my family, but now he wasn't there to make things right. Instead of things seeming just a little bit better they were the opposite.

I'd wake up in the middle of night and the house would be eerily quiet. The kind of silence where you could sense it was the early hours of the morning. The lack of sound meant Mom must still be out. I didn't blame her for going out all the time, for drinking away the agony whenever her memory recalled her son. I know our pain was different, but it shared the same intensity, and we had different ways of relieving it. Hers was to disappear altogether. She lost herself in alcohol. Johnny's death fuelled her alcoholism to a new level. While I could understand the reasons behind it, it didn't lessen the hurt. I felt forgotten and abandoned. *She still had me, wasn't I good enough for her? Did she wish it was me that died, instead of him?* These were questions I was never brave enough to ask her. They remained the thoughts that ran through my mind whenever she forgot to pick me up from school, or cook dinner, or tell me she loved me.

While I'd lie awake and wait to hear her come in the door, anger would boil up inside me.

'How could you do this to us?' I'd catch myself speaking the words I was thinking. 'I need you so much and you're not here. You should be here!'

The soft words grew louder and louder and before I knew I'd be yelling. All the rage I couldn't express to those living around me was directed to him. He took on everything, but this time he wasn't there to make things brighter.

'Are you listening?! I said you should be here! Why did you do this to me? This is all your fault!'

I paused for a moment. Silence. I almost expected to hear a reply. When nothing came, the tears started.

'I'm sorry! I didn't mean. Just please come back. Please!' I thought if I pleaded enough, by some miracle he'd be back in my life and everything would return to normal. I admit I still have these days. Old enough to know better, but still holding on to the wishes of a child.

Even being older and wiser hasn't stopped me from experiencing the same fears I went through many years ago. I'm more capable of refuting them now, but they still creep into my mind on occasions.

When I wasn't blaming Johnny, I was wondering if it was something I had done. If I had been a better sister, daughter, whatever – maybe he would still be here. I thought back to all the times we fought, all the times I'd argue with him or pester him or call him names. Normal occurrences between siblings but they left me feeling guilty. Maybe it was my fault.

'You broke it!'
'I'm sorry. I was just trying to help you.'
'Who asked you to?'
'You did!'
'I didn't ask you to break it!'
'Fine. Don't ever ask me for another favor, you little brat!'
'I hate you! I wish I never had a brother!'

It is clear in my memory. I told him I hated him. I wished he never existed. Neither was true, but I still spoke those words. What if that was what he remembered as he was dying? After the bullet struck his chest and he fell to the ground, thoughts of our mom, dad, sister and me circling around his mind and what if when he got to me, he heard my voice telling him I hated him? I'd pray it wasn't true. I prayed he recalled all the times we raced and he let me win, or the time he and my dad built the stable for my new pony, telling me it was a chicken coop. And the look on my face when I ran in the house to tell him there was a horse in the chicken coop. I never forgot the look on his as he laughed at me. As I'd list the joyful experiences, my thoughts would drift further from the guilt even if just for a short time.

Those are the memories I cherish the most. The ones that aren't connected to the hard times but are simply about having a wonderful older brother. It's impossible to think of those without the constant reminder that he's not here anymore. I will always have that part of me that aches for him, but through the years I have become adapt to smiling in spite of it.

It's the best I can hope for and finally I can be strong enough for both of us.

Calshot Light

Naomi K. Bagel

They sat in silence. The sort of silence that is easy and companionable, the space created by their lack of words was filled with the sound of seagulls, which shrieked as they wheeled and turned. Against the side of the small clinker-built wooden fishing boat the waves slapped constantly and regularly.

Alfie thought how ageless the moment was. Those waves that were striking this night against the side of the 'Boy Jack' were all part of that timeless ocean crossed by small currachs that had put to sea years ago, centuries ago, with nothing but stretched cowhide making the barrier between the watery depths and keeping alive. The tides had continued over generations to work their ebb and flow over the very same water that had been crossed by fearsome Viking long ships and then of course there were those Romans. They had come in their legions, bearing stinging nettles, syphilis and snails as gifts.

Alfie pulled himself out of his reverie. It was getting on

towards midnight, and as the helmsman he couldn't be spacing off like that. Not even with the boat chugging quietly along in the lee of the Calshot light vessel. It was Alfie's boat and it was his responsibility to keep an eye out for other shipping. He was punching the tide two miles out from the shores with the lights of Calshot Spit twinkling and the shape of the old fort showing clearly in the full moon. It was important not to drift off.

Stocky and swarthy, Alfie was a distinctive character. His thick dark curls and bushy beard furnished him with a rather unkempt appearance but this wild man persona was balanced by a soft Dorset voice, lively blue eyes and a ready smile. Well wrapped up on this chill April evening, the thick body hair that had given rise to the name Bear was visible above the neckline of the grubby Arran jumper that he wore. A Dorset man, Alfie knew this coast well. It was the territory that he was familiar with since the days of his early childhood when his father had taken him out in a small sailing dinghy round Poole Harbour.

Alfie loved his fishing boat; the beat of the single cylinder diesel engine could be heard echoing back from the mud walls that formed the entrance to the Beaulieu banks. Although in tune with the sea and its tides, Alfie was not comfortable with that small echo. It reminded him all too clearly of his wife, the pregnant and faithless Lindy, and brought his mind back to those moments six years ago when he loved her. How he loved to sit and play his guitar while watching the naked Lindy lying on their bed methodically rubbing some sort of oily stuff into her swollen belly. Sometimes he would stop playing, and kneel beside her, to place an ear to the heartbeat of that new life hidden deep in her body. His child-to-be, that he was predestined never to meet because the faithless Lindy left with her first love, Tom, a month before the child, their child, *his* child was born.

They went to Scotland and out of his life. The divorce papers were long done and dusted. So there was Alfie, a father who had never seen his child, a husband without a wife. Not the sort of things to dwell too deeply upon, and that philosophy was reinforced by the way that the folks down the pub dealt with his divorce.

'Never mind, Bear, there's plenty more fish in the sea!' said the captain of the bar billiards team as he placed a brimming pint in front of Alfie and slapped him on the back. 'Plenty more fish in the sea,' echoed the chap sitting on the bar stool next to them. 'Plenty more fish! That's a good one!'

Alfie smiled and drank his beer, unaware that his smile was like the red pennant that jauntily flew from the foredeck of his boat, cheerfully belying the fact that deep in the bilges murky water and leaden weights lurked.

'Get that down you lad. There's not much in life that good ale can't cure.'

'You're right,' said Alfie and drained his glass.

'Good old Bear,' his mates said. 'He's not the boy to let things get him down.'

So Alfie downed another beer and signed up for the tug of war team in the carnival. His pals cheered loudly. Someone called for a song while another chap put a guitar into Alfie's hands and soon his clear voice was leading the singing.

Like the Mary Ellen Carter rise again... rise again...

There seemed to be neither time nor point in dwelling too deeply on the faithless Lindy and the love and commitment that he had given to her. The deep stirring of emotion that prospective paternity had awakened was now directionless and had frozen hard within him. He couldn't bear to think about it, it was too painful, far too much hurt. After she left he built a bonfire which had consumed in its cleansing flames every piece of material evidence of the time spent with Lindy.

Alfie's love of his boat and the hours at sea satisfied his spirit and he recognised that in the timeless space when he was alone he would become whole again, one man, working with the elements, in the same way the ancestors had done. Alone on the sea Alfie's soul could merge so close to the ancient spirits that at times he felt his breathing fall into tune with the rhythm of the waves. The songs that he sang to the sea and the sky were a distillation of that oneness.

He couldn't trust women anymore, and that path to his soul that Lindy had explored and exploited was sealed, not to be opened again. Alfie knew that there was no room for any female to get too close to him ever again in his life. To his surprise an easy friendship had developed with Jan, a quiet woman who worked in the harbour café, and somehow they had drifted into a relationship that answered the hunger in his body in an undemanding way. They didn't speak much about personal things, that wasn't in the remit of their friendship. They spent the time that they chose to be together in the pub or in bed, and sometimes they would go out on the boat mutually drifting an evening away in an undemanding silence.

Tonight was different.

'Look at all those stars,' Jan said, putting her hand out to touch Alfie. 'So clear. Just look – there's The Milky Way... Orion's Belt... The Big Bear and The Little Bear....' Alfie felt a chill inside him and moved away.

'Come on,' said Jan, flinging her arms around Alfie. 'Let's have a bit of a cuddle before we set off home.'

Close to her, he was lost in the sexuality and urgency of the moment.

'You make a cuppa then and I'll find the best place to drop anchor. I'll join you below deck when I'm done.'

'Righto,' said Jan blowing him a kiss. Two miles offshore and guided by the deep channel markers, he cut the engine and dropped anchor, watching the great length of chain snake down into the dark waters.

The sounds of waves and sea birds were overlaid by their noisy lovemaking. Afterwards Alfie pulled his clothes on.

'Do you have to?' asked Jan putting a hand out.

'Yes, I need to bring the boat home.'

'I've been thinking...'

Alfie laced up his deck shoes as Jan, still naked, moved closer towards him.

'Maybe, we should move in together.'

He froze. There were no words he could find to answer her.

'Maybe we could do more things together?'

He could hear her voice but to reply became an impossibility. He picked up his guitar and as his fingers made chords he strove to express that feeling, the shape and power of his emotions that had no words, only sounds. As he played, music from his soul filled the cabin. He tried to master this turmoil, in the same way that he was able to master the sea.

'*There's nothing left of me to give*,' he sang and then became aware that Jan was dressed.

'More tea?' she asked.

Alfie nodded and laid down his guitar.

'I didn't want you to stop playing. It sounded nice.'

'Tell you what,' he said, 'if you want to pull the anchor up I'll bring my guitar on deck.'

44

'Great,' she said.

The moonlight flecked the dark waters with silver, and outlined Jan's figure as she stood on the foredeck, bent over to the anchor chain. Alfie moved towards her and pressed his hands gently on her lower back. Everything he wanted to say gained power and, lacking any verbal outlet, it became physical. With his hands against her back, he pushed, and was surprised with the ease that she fell into the water. He heard her shout, but there was no reply. He stowed the anchor, started the engine, set and lashed the helm for the open sea, then picked up his guitar and sang.

There's nothing left of me to give,
I'm spent, exhausted, broken,
No poetry can save the day,
A verse, a line, a token.
For I set sail with fastened helm,
The course could not be altered,
I never saw those blasted rocks,
On which I sadly faltered.
But strange enough, I didn't drown,
I simply sat here freezing.
No mermaids came to rescue me,
All I could hear was breathing.
Alive, I know there's no escape,
I'll have to watch the sea.
And nothing's there but sea and rocks,
And rocks and sea and me.

Majoni and the Talisman

Tinashe Mushakavanhu

Senga is a township where nothing much ever happens. We live in mute faceless matchboxes, rows of similar houses following dusty roads snaking like bulging veins on an emaciated body. Our houses are so close. There is no privacy. We are one big communal family. We hate any people among us who think they are important. We talk behind their backs with awful scorn. They make butter for our daily bread of gossip. Perhaps you could say township dwellers have an envious pull-him-down tendency, an intolerance of excelling individuals. We tear them down; we reduce them to the same level of general mediocrity as the rest of us.

It is in this vein that people talked about a certain man, who has come to be known by the generic name – Majoni. He was a huge burly man, strong as a baobab tree and lived in the big L-shaped house in Ngulube Street. He had a lovely wife, three children and a respectable job at a local bank. He drove a beautiful car, a silver-grey Peugeot 402, the only one of its kind in the township, perhaps even in the city. But fortune had not always smiled at him.

He started life just like any other half-starved homeless orphan. He had struggled his way to university and soon afterwards became a bank teller and rose to become a manager. What more could a man want? A wife and children – that he already had. To someone like Majoni who had a struggling start, money was the root of life. Money was the serpent in the Garden of Eden. It slithered into his mind, tempted him to taste a little more of it until his mind was overtaken by the desire to own more of it. Majoni became a willing victim of the sweet-talking serpent. 'Majoni don't starve yourself of the pleasures of the world that money can bring,' the serpent said. 'When you have more money you are a king, you have unlimited choices and like God you begin to own everything.' Majoni could not resist the tempting fruit.

Whenever people assume a 'new' status, they separate themselves from the rest of us. They erect high dura-walls round their yards to protect their families from our prying eyes. Their affluence is masked in stern faces. It is obscenely stencilled on black zinc gates:

CHENJERAI IMBWA
BEWARE OF DOGS

And yet there are no islands in the township. No one has much of a private life. Townships are big, big entities. Neighbours curiously peek over their low fences to see what is happening next door. We make it our business to know all about each other. We mind each other's business as neighbours should. It is not our fault. It is the historical legacy of *hunhuism*, of living together. Now, those who choose to be private often become the

47

threading wool of our rumour mill. We speculate about them.

The story was that Majoni had made a great trip to Joza, the lingo name for Johannesburg, to see a *sangoma*[1], as it is a popular belief that South African *sangomas* have strong *muti*[2] for individuals to make a lot of money. Everyone knows this story, or at least, some version of it. The *sangoma* prepared the *muti* for Majoni but for the medicine to work he had to sacrifice three people he loved most. Once he accepted the conditions Majoni was told the pact was binding. Eternal. Those who broke their pacts, he was warned, were assailed by hallucinations and haunted by things without names. They would not die but as punishment the wires in their heads would short circuit and go crazy and lead sad, destitute lives. Majoni was given a small black bag. He was told to put food into the bag and never try to see what was inside. Do that everyday and you will be fine, you will have all the money you want, the *sangoma* instructed Majoni. People say the black bag was a goblin. People talk, never knowing for sure if the goblin existed. No one has actually seen it; it probably explains our collective paranoia. Perhaps we imagine phantoms to keep our minds from the hunger and poverty that marks our lives.

So according to township legend that is how Majoni acquired his wealth and got endless promotions at work. As it were the goblin did not like sharing Majoni's affection with his children. The goblin would terrorize the children by scratching them while they were sleeping, leaving long, parallel scratches on their backs and in the insides of their thighs. One by one the children died in bizarre accidents. The first was run over by a car. The second drowned in the bath-tub. And the third, a baby boy, died of a mysterious disease, some say it was mumps or measles. But whatever it was

1. medicine man
2. traditional medicine

that had nipped Majoni's children in the bud, people turned up for the funerals in large numbers not because they cared but because they wanted to be inside the house everyone talked about and see for themselves and verify stories making the rounds. Once at the funeral, people forgot their 'spy missions' and got absorbed in the food. There was always lots of food. At least, they would get to erase the hunger that hounded their lives. Up to this day, people talk about these funerals as 'funeral weddings' because of the food. *Chenjerai masalad aya asikana, mungaite manyoka.*[3] *Asikana wedzerai nyama handisi kuda* cabbage *ini.*[4] *Pambotengwa makreti manganiko?*[5] *Hona kutanga kufeeder hama dzavo* first?[6] *Vanhu ava vanoziva chakadya mwana, hamuone maitiro avo*[7]. *Mukadzi wacho kuwanza* make-up *kani.*[8]

Unlike other township women who spent their days sewing, knitting or vending at street corners, Majoni's wife did nothing. Some say Majoni's wife had become the goblin's mistress. Goblins make love to their mistresses and in return rewarded with milk and food. Majoni's wife would spend the day lying on the sofa giving the housemaid endless tasks. Yes, they had a paid house worker – Sisi Mejuri. *Shuwa nekuoma kwakaita zvinhu mazuva ano ndiani anokwanisa musikana webasa?*[9] There was no end to the speculation.

And yet no one ever saw the goblin. It remained a mystery. Sisi Mejuri never saw it either. Occasionally she would hear a loud, slow 'clump! clump!' as though somebody was walking on the

---

3. Avoid salads, you will have diarrhoea.
4. I don't want any cabbage, more meat please.
5. How many crates of soft drinks are available?
6. Look, it's the relatives who get food first.
7. Look how they are behaving, they know what ate the children?
8. Look at all the make-up with Majoni's wife.
9. With the way things are these days who can afford to employ a housemaid?

roof. Some days they would wake up to find their bodies smeared with Vaseline and other concoctions. Even more bizarrely, they would wake up to find themselves outside the house.

Sisi Mejuri remembered days she would see an old man wearing a thick winter coat, and a hat concealing parts of his face. He had protruding reddish monkey ears, a hairy face. It was the face of an old man on a boy's body. He was a queer sort of human being. He never said anything. He never laughed. There was something spooky about his appearance. It was probably the way he carried himself, this natural restraint from all things human. No one knew who he was or if he ever existed except Majoni and his wife. He has remained a mystery to this day.

Then Majoni and his wife had started having fights, real fights, and those peculiar marital disagreements. They started throwing furniture at each other, and dragging up past grievances. Why are you coming home late? There is lots of work. No, you are seeing someone else; you have a 'small house' somewhere. Jealous bitch. And on and on the arguments would go. They would start as mild disagreements that would fizzle down like Diet Coke, but they became more heated and explosive. The problem with *muti* money is that it never brings happiness. It is selfish and wreaks havoc. It breaks families apart. It kills. Each morning, Majoni and his wife would wake up with bruised eyes, missing teeth, charred hands, torn finger nails, scratch marks until one fateful morning when Majoni's wife was discovered by Sisi Mejuri collapsed on the bedroom floor. And there had been blood and bank notes on the floor, everywhere. Afterwards Sisi Mejuri quit her job. Some say she went back to her rural areas. She complained of being beaten by invisible things. And sometimes she would get up in the morning to find her bedding mysteriously wet, signs that someone had had sex with her the night before. Things she could not recall.

50

Township dwellers had a different story. It was Majoni's goblin. Township gossip makes for the best form of news. It is more entertaining, instant, dramatic, detailed and intimate than BBC or CNN can ever be. Township women know how to sniff out a story, in a person's dressing, in the way a girl concealing pregnancy walks or behaves, they can tell a cracking marriage in the rows of green, pink, yellow houses. They can diagnose AIDS or TB. And they are often not wrong. They had a story in Majoni's family. Poor woman, they said. How did she put up with that monster of a man? So the township women took turns to visit her in hospital, bringing her food, offering her messages of solidarity. Yet the women only wanted to be at the ringside, to witness first hand the Majoni family drama. Majoni was often the object of scrutiny. The air reeked of outrage. And anger. And scandal. And suspicion. Mountains of accusations ranged through the minds of the women until the earthquake of those infernal thoughts cracked in the form of whispers. *Asikana*[10], did you see how that man is acting. *Chirume ichi hachinyare shuwa, mweya wetsvina chete*[11]. We knew that man is no good from the first day he came to live in this township.

He came from nowhere, built this big house and never made efforts to make friends. Majoni was the kind of person who had no idea who his neighbours were. *Munhu wepi asingataudzane nevavakidzani vake?*[12] We speculated. *Zvikwambo izvi. Hameno magame aari kutamba kubasa. Hamuzivi here kuti muzukuru waPresident*.[13] All three possibilities were likely. Since the

---

10. Ladies
11. Look at this shameless man, he is demonic.
12. What kind of person is he who does not have words with his neighbours?
13. Maybe he has goblins. Maybe he is involved in some corrupt activities at work? Maybe he is the president's nephew.

ruinous land invasions of 2000, these were the only choices available to people, their lives were a thesaurus of desperate choices, use of *zvikwambo*, nepotism, corruption, prostitution, bribery, misery, AIDS. Nothing legal could keep anyone alive or beat the insane ways of inflation. Prices were going up everyday and yet salaries remained rooted like the Nyanga mountains. Only a man like Jesus could say to a mountain, hey you, move over there, I am tired of seeing you at the same spot everyday. None of us, including our leaders, had mountain-moving faith like Jesus. We lived our lives according to the dictates of convenience. So when Majoni's wife became mysteriously ill, there was this hullabaloo in the township. Majoni's things had beaten his wife. Majoni's things had eaten his children.

Some of the religious women in the township set to convert Majoni and his wife. *Mhuri iyi inoda Jesu chete*[14]. Easy converts are found in hospitals, last minute converts. People can question the existence of God but no one can come to terms with the possibility of spending eternity in Gehena. Majoni's wife easily converted to one of those overzealous Pentecostal churches. She condemned the ways of the past. One of the church people even brought her a present of a T-shirt written: THE PAST IS A FOREIGN COUNTRY. She became a new person.

Now, *muti* and God do not mix. The first time the church women visited Majoni's wife after she was discharged from the hospital, strange things happened in the house. Hysterical noises and indecipherable voices echoed in the house. Lights flickered on and off. Chicken feet dripping with blood dropped from the roof. Household objects were lifted and thrown about by invisible beings; insulting writing appeared on the walls, the praying women were spat at, and there was a lot of swearing and cursing.

14. This family needs Jesus, needs salavation.

Windows rattled as if there was an earth tremor. A strong spell had surrounded the house. Then suddenly everything was quiet, a silence as loud as a shout. The women continued praying and crying and pleading with God.

After that, nobody knows what happened. Perhaps the 'daemons' had been exorcised and gone into the Gadarene swine. Wires in Majoni's head crossed. He lost his job. Since Majoni could no longer manage to buy petrol on the black-market, his car stopped running. First, he sold the wheels, then another part and another and another. The body of the Peugeot 402 became a chicken run. Majoni's wife became a fervent church-goer *wekwa* Johane Masowe.[15] She became a popular prophetess. She could pray for people using healing water and cooking oil. She refused to be paid or if she was paid she shared all her lot with her neighbours or anyone in the township in need. Her reputation of healing went far and wide. Some of her clients were the pig-like snorting ministers; the Pierre Cardin suited business people, headmasters, teachers, footballers, nurses.

No one really knows what happened to the goblin. Some say the goblin entered Majoni's body and caused chaos in his mind. Something went wrong in his mind. It seemed a sewerage pipe burst in there. And a rushing turmoil had drenched everything in Majoni's mind. Majoni became a non-believer. He became so disillusioned that he lost all purpose in life. He refused to be a member of his wife's church. People in the township said he was now paying for making money through dark ways. He started sleeping everywhere, under footbridges, at the council beer hall, at the door steps of shops, everywhere.

***

15. belonging to the Johane Masowe apostolic sect

Majoni is the old man you see when you come to our township sitting at the bottle store, wearing a pair of torn Tenderfoots with peeping toes, parched trousers, unkempt hair, lice-infested clothes, an unwashed body mapped with sores. His face is long and haggard, scarred by the many struggles he has faced. He is that man who has lived all his life picking fags, demanding change from school children and housewives running errands at the market. No one knows where Majoni came from.

Solstice Crab

Guinevere Clark

He came round with a giant cooking pot. I felt like Alice in Wonderland.

'Go on then,' I said, lifting my chin to the silver circle, 'what's in your pot?'

He opened the lid with a boy look, my eyes got wider and wider. I felt like a mother to my lover. Slowly it was exposed, a huge, frisbee-sized crab, the biggest I'd ever seen. I thought it was dead, a specimen, a glimpse of what belongs in the great, green sink of our sea. Then, all of a sudden, its fat front pincer reached out with a stiff and desperate lethargy.

'Oh', I squawked, 'it's still alive!'

He'd been handed the crab in a plastic bag by a young boy who'd been swinging it round, like an interesting toy. The summer was at its peak, beaches and havens were thick with random fishermen, fluke catches and – at twilight – always the hardened men who stood like sculptures on the edge, their lines invisible.

'No one will let me cook it,' he protested. I drew in a sharp breath.

'Well, if it was dead and, and small, or maybe if we were flat with hunger, maybe.'

'It is dead,' he said.

'Not quite,' I shouted.

We deliberated, debated, dug deep into the rights and wrongs of the crab's death. It sat, motionless, stripped of its second front pincer. Beyond that last surge, now there was just stillness, a sea Buddha bereft of its temple.

'Oh God, I can't take this, a crab facing its final moments in the strip lights of my kitchen.' He didn't apologise.

Not so far back it was a crusted knight, surely the master of its maze. It was strong and old, years and years old, but not quite as old as a crab can get. He looked like he'd fathered many children, danced with his kin, pirouetting in the soft, hard sand clouds. Movement – a distant memory of protection as he squats now, like a magnificent shell.

He thought it best to cook it, placed that great pan on the hob, poured and poured the salt in. People over compensate when there is something inherently wrong.

'At least light a candle for it', I demanded, overcome with weakness. He lit two. The solstice was yesterday and the moon had hung and still hung in Cancer. It seemed to me like the stars had crumbled and landed in my kitchen. The great crab, the keeper of home and family was here, washed up at my door.

We hovered over the pot; he lay fixed as a fossil, bubbles gently breaking beneath him. It was late. I imagined what mission this massive crab was on last night, as the moon broke her many beams on the sea's webbed floor. Perhaps if he'd climbed a different path, was pushed on a softer wave, not let his claw be caught so coldly from the shore, he'd still be gracing the depths. Now, like some macabre spell, he's the focus of our quiet – half bathing, half dying, I'm not sure which. I felt sick, sick from the smell of old sea and the day's heat and that crab's liminal stare.

Then it moved, not just a bit of it, all of it, for a second. A weak launch from those hinged legs. I screamed like a gull and I screamed again.

'Stop cooking it, stop cooking it, I'm taking it back to the sea.'

'Okay', he said swiftly and blew out the candles in a tight breath.

I pulled on my wellies under my nightdress. He sealed the pot like a coffin. We scurried to the door and drove in silence to the shore. The tide was as far away as it can get. We paced out with the pot, its lukewarm water weighing heavy as guilt. Under a rock's watery crook he set it, like an ornament in the dark. There wasn't a moon. I cracked my lighter till my finger burnt, just to see him flicker, but he didn't.

Then, just once through the dark, from his hidden face, two neon dots cut thinly through the pool, like a tiny machine loosing its pulse. I blessed it as much as I could in my long white nightdress, mysterious blue in this moonless place.

At the car we looked out at the endless navy. No sea to be seen, just the silhouettes of those huge Gemini cliffs, mothering the crux of the beach.

Concealment

Liz Hambley

I look out.

I strain my eyes to see. It's quite a distance considering my eyesight. I should really wear my glasses. Can I be bothered to fetch them? Will I miss whatever is out there if I leave my spot? I'm wedged in my chair in the corner of the bedroom. This gives me a good view without being seen from outside. I know this because I've tried it out.

I've seen him, once. I've seen a bit of him anyway. The rest was obscured by black. Black trousers, shoes and a hoody. His face was partly concealed by camouflage paint. I dreamt him of course. I always dream things before they happen. He's been there for months but no one will take me seriously. The police humour me but I know what they think.

Most of my waking hours are spent in the bedroom looking for just a glimpse. I only move to eat and go to the toilet. I don't have dinners, just a quick sandwich. Even when it's dark

I'm looking. I've seen a burst of light once maybe from a cigarette lighter. The only street light is by the bridge that leads to the river, under the main road. He is careful to keep out of the light preferring the bank hidden in the undergrowth. The council used to keep it down but cutbacks have stopped all that. I started to trim it once but I was stopped by a council workman who told me I couldn't do it and muttered something about not being covered by insurance if I got hurt. The cheek. They don't realise what danger I'm in.

I only go out twice a week now. Once to do a little bit of shopping and once to do my shift with the Samaritans. People say the saddest things, but it is nice to be of help. Apart from that I'm always in. Always in, watching for him. My friends rarely bother to come and see me these days. They do phone of course, but we seem to have so little in common now.

Listen to me going on. What's the time? Half-past two in the morning, no wonder the sensation has gone from my legs. Perhaps I should get a better chair. Recliner, like you see on the telly. Have I blown my chance? Nothing moves on the bank. I should go to bed, though of course I find it hard to sleep what with the dreams. Nightmares really. Though I can't always remember them when I am awake.

Mostly I lead a pretty ordinary life and the next few days are no exception. I see no one and I see nothing on the bank. My weight is plummeting probably since I seem to have less time to eat now than before. I need a bath but I'm so busy and I'm not sure I can spare the time; there is no one here to smell me anyway. I hear the postman. The BT logo stares out at me and I can't believe it's my phone bill already. Look at that, almost four times higher than usual. Four times! Something must be wrong and I need to speak to the phone company.

I spend nearly two hours on the phone to BT getting absolutely nowhere. They are adamant that all the calls have been made from my phone. It turns out they are all chat line numbers. They ask the usual questions and I explain that nobody lives with me and I don't phone chat lines. Then I realise when I get my diary that all the calls look like they have been made when I'm not in. Now surely the police will listen to me.

The burly heavy-eyed policeman on duty at the counter seems to remember me and I'm sure I see him wince. I show him the bill and my diary to prove I was out at the time when the calls were made. He doesn't believe me. I can see by his eyes. 'Have you considered placing a block on premium line numbers?' he suggests in that tone that they all have.

Later that night it hits me that the man in black must have been in my house. Or had he been able to hack into my phone line from another location? I've read about that kind of thing. I phoned a couple of friends to try and find out if this could be so but they were non-committal and very reticent to answer me. I was up at my window again as soon as I could. Looking out trying to see if he was there. I needed to know.

I hear a car pulling up and I looked down. It's familiar and I am surprised to see some colleagues of mine from the Samaritans. They are an unnecessary distraction but not wishing to be rude I welcome them in. Jenny who I like to think of as my friend asks, 'Are you alright?' I can see the rest look at me with worried expressions. I'm sure I was doing a shift with Jenny at the time of one of the calls. Will she remember?

My hands are shaking. She studies the now crumpled bill but her face is blank and I feel my heart drop. She looks up and I can see her face is drained of any colour. She whispers to the others, 'We were out all day that day. I remember it well

60

because we were out looking for a birthday present for you, Alan. You remember?'

'Are you sure?' he asks.

'Yes, I can prove we were. Let me find my debit card slips.' I watch her as she empties out her purse. Small receipts spew out over the table and she rifles through them. 'There, this one. Look – it gives the date and time we were there.'

We compare it and surely now there is no doubt that my phone has been used by someone else. I can prove he exists and I am elated. Someone has to believe me.

They stay with me for a while. We even have a nice cuppa. I no longer feel it's a waste of my time them being here. I show them where I sit for hours at my window looking out. Alan offers to go down to the bank, although it's raining. Such a nice man. We all watch him from the window to the point where he disappears and we see him return and let him in, eager to hear from him. He explains there is no one there but there is a spot that is worn out on the bank which could be from someone lying down watching. And there is other proof: used cigarette ends littering the grass and two empty cans of coke. He has picked some up for evidence, muttering about DNA. I feel happier than I have done for ages. I am believed at last. My friends apologise for doubting me.

By the time they leave it is almost eleven, but I'm not deterred and I sit in my chair, in the bedroom, to start my vigil. Keeping awake is a problem as I sit in silence and it takes time for my eyes to accustom themselves to the change in light. There is only a slight hint of yellow where there should be a moon and the clouds hide any pin prick of stars. I try not look at my watch and time drags but suddenly I see one movement and then another. I hear a shout and I see someone

61

get up and run but it happens so quickly and is over so soon that I haven't really seen anything. I see people waving at me and I take a second look. Alan and Jenny are out there so I go downstairs to let them in.

Still worried, they had come back to check out my bank. Alan says he saw my man but had been unable to catch him. Jenny thinks she may have seen something but she is unsure. I beg them not to do it again. I have no idea if my man is dangerous. Alan asks me if I want him to stay the night. I reply I don't, my man won't be back tonight. Surely he'd have been scared off. Alan and Jenny go and I allow myself time off. I watch TV. Some light entertainment might take my mind off things. I sleep well except for one bad dream which I can't quite remember.

I feel good in the morning, relieved now I know some people no longer think me crazy. I actually want to go out to get food and I may treat myself to some new clothes, or shoes. I phone Jenny to see if she will join me and I'm very happy she agrees to meet in town. I prolong the day for as long as possible by having lunch out for the first time in ages. The new café near the station does some lovely baguettes. As I drive home, carrier bags on the seat next to mine, I can't help feeling a sense of relief.

I open the front door and stagger into the kitchen with my bags, dropping them all on the table whilst I go to put the kettle on. It is hot like it's not long been boiled and something catches my eye. There is a dirty cup in the sink. Shakily I phone Jenny to tell her. She offers to come round. But maybe I'm over-reacting. It's only a cup after all.

I start my vigil again as soon as I can but I see nothing. I decide to have a bath and I try and lie back in its warmth to relax but I can only do that for so long before my mind starts to work overtime again. Still I feel better as I dry myself off and I enter the bedroom to get my nightwear. The drawer is stiff; something seems stuck down the back. All my pants have been pulled about. The cup was one thing, but I know I haven't done this. He has been here. I begin to remember my dream. I can't breathe. I start sobbing uncontrollably. I do not know what to do as I cannot involve Jenny or any of the other women and Alan; the only man who is a close friend is bound to be busy at work. What could I tell him anyway? Not what I had seen in my dream.

It is getting dark now. The phone ringing makes a welcome break but I don't quite reach it before the answer-phone kicks in. A voice comes on the line, a husky robotic voice. It's him and he's talking to me. '*You have interesting underwear. I want to see you wear it. I want to get in your head my lovely.*' I grab the phone but as I do he hangs up. I snatch the tape out of the machine. I know the importance of evidence now. I wanted to ask him, why me? But I couldn't and now I'm determined that he will be punished. I decide to go to bed just to defy him but I do take a rounders bat which I place under the pillow next to me, just in case. Despite everything I do fall asleep but I wake every hour. I keep an eye on the clock but it all seems quiet. I am surprised to finally wake at nearly nine. It takes me a while to come to but as I look around my room something seems to be wrong. Then I see what. Yesterdays pants are draped over my mirror and written in red lipstick are the words, *You smell divine*! My bra is draped over the foot of my bed.

The police must listen now. I spend an age explaining who I am and what it's about. They go to get my previous notes. It seems an age before they come back but they do, eventually. I have proof now. Grudgingly the policeman says he will send someone in a car to look. I busy myself getting showered and dressed all the time careful not to touch the evidence. I wait and wait but no one shows. I phone again and they assure me someone will come but I have to wait my turn as there is more pressing crime being committed. I cannot for the life of me think what could be more pressing, except perhaps murder. I almost give up when I receive a phone call from the police asking me if my problem can wait till tomorrow. They ask if he has physically or verbally threatened me. I'm unsure how to answer this so I explain it all again. They push me to one side deciding that he won't risk coming back again tonight. I am not convinced but I have to accept it. I have no choice. I borrow Jenny's dog Nipper, a Jack Russell. Better than the police any day.

Night comes again. I have gone over everything in my mind so many times and I still can't make any sense of it. I am so tired. The deep growling noise reminds me Nipper is curled at my feet. I tell him to be quiet and he obeys but he is alert to every sound and is watching my every move. I creep out of bed and hide behind the door. I don't have long to wait. I hear noises. Are they from the bathroom? Is he going through my dirty washing again? Suddenly, so quietly that I never hear him coming, he opens my door. I am ready with my rounders bat but before I can get there the dog flies at him. He tries to fend him off but by now I am hitting his legs as hard as I can. He screams out, an almost inhuman noise. The dog is going for his throat now he is on his knees. I hit him anywhere I can. Some blows land on his head which has started to bleed. And his hands are bleeding too where he has tried to fend off the dog. His black mask is ripped but not enough for me to see his face. My final blow renders him unconscious. I rush to ring the police. This time they take me seriously. I take no chances. I get several pairs of tights, from my drawer, and tie up his hands and feet. Apart

64

from that I am too frightened to touch him in case he comes to life. His blood is staining my carpet but I don't care. I hold the dog to calm him, all the time speaking to him soothingly. I feel him relax. I wish I could.

I hear the sirens. I glance over at my man in black. Is he stirring? I chance a trip down to open the door for the police as I don't want them to break the door. Why on earth I worry about a bloody door I don't know. There is a huge crash as the man comes through my bedroom door. He is holding my rounders bat and aiming it at me. I struggle to hold the dog. I fall, afraid for me and the dog. I scream at the two policemen to do something. They are ready for him with their batons. He is cut to the ground as he receives more blows to the head. He doesn't get up again, but to be sure he is handcuffed. I am ushered out of the hallway and I go to sit in the lounge. An ambulance is called and he is taken away. After the police leave I realise I still have not seen the face of my attacker.

The next day I go to the police station to give a statement. I still have no idea who this man in black is. Jenny came with me to keep me company and I was glad she had. I am burning to ask the question but first they make me dictate my statement. I am asked if I have any idea who it is. I have none. Then the policeman, who came last night, tells me that it is someone I know. I am shown his picture. I gasp. Jenny takes the photo from my hand.

'It can't be – it's Alan.'

I remain friends with Jenny. I have bought myself a new comfy chair and some days we chat for hours on the phone. I don't have nightmares. I have my own dog now, and nothing to fear.

Nothing to fear.

Valldemossa

Tyler Guthrie

It's a sound I cannot imitate and a moment difficult to capture in any light. Something startled them, one became excited, or they simply decided to part. A flutter later and the birds are gone.

It's Tuesday, or Wednesday, I don't really remember which. There's Mass everyday and I haven't looked at a calendar for three weeks. It doesn't really matter. I worked briefly this morning before going to *Forn Valldemossa* for a stale croissant and acrid coffee. It's always shit; there aren't many options in paradise.

There's a table next to the door where I sit when I can. It overlooks the valley below Valldemossa, the same valley that stirred Sand and crippled Chopin. Today it is full of Germans. I had to sit at the other wall and peek past the thick tourists to see the birds.

'Kann ich ihnen helfen?'

Probably not. I'm trying to catch the birds.

'Catch the birds. Right. Where are you from? Not many of

us tourists this time of year, no.'

I'm not a tourist. I winter here. The other two at the table spoke to each other in German, the fat one made me angry. Tourists ruin this place. Only in the winter is it real. When I arrived, the last of the tourists were leaving – thank God. Coming back from the *cerveceria* the first night, I saw an American on the balcony of his rental, apparently he locked himself out. He was drunk, most likely cold and stupid. He was still there in the morning wrapped in deck pillows tied with a clothes line. I'm not sure what he did with his shoes, but in the morning they were resting in a tree just out of reach.

'So, you are an American?'

This damn question, I hate hearing it. A confirmation always seems to lead to one of two responses; a condescending 'oh' followed by a strained attempt at a congenial association i.e. 'my second cousin lived in the States for a year' or the inevitable follow up question, 'What do *you* think of Mr Bush?' Regardless of my answer I then get lectured on why the United States is arrogant and Americans ignorant.

I'm Canadian.

'Oh.' Surprised. 'So, what do you think of Mr Bush?'

The Germans asked several more questions about me and where they should go. I left quickly. I wanted my table, I wanted my space, and I wanted to be left alone.

The work I started earlier wasn't productive. It was shadows and lighting. Trying to keep the light on as it were. I'm fraught in my work. Katie tries to help but never can. I'd call her my mistress or possibly my muse but she is neither. She is British and rich. I went over to her flat at noon and she was crying. He father was calling her home.

'I don't understand how he can do this. He said a year and

67

it's only been two months.' She was supposed to be working. She left home an Eco-tourist and she'll go back a sedentary tart.

I took her over to the sofa and held her, I tried to speak words of comfort but I didn't know any. All I could recall were old girlfriends and broken promises. We stayed on the sofa for two hours; she drifted off to sleep in my arms while I drifted off into the valley.

Before I left Katie's, I witnessed the single most entertaining event in Spain. A little black and white bird, no taller than a deck of cards, marched past the open French doors of the flat. It came from the left behind the wall with his legs jutting out far in front of him as he strode across the balcony. As his right foot planted itself in the middle of the doorway, he glanced over at me and froze – he was shocked and what I will call embarrassed. He turned and bolted back the way he came with his little legs marching at a frantic pace. A second later he ran across the door again, bent on whatever it was that originally caught his fancy. I was amused.

I returned to the bakery hoping to reclaim my window and the valley below. It's not a compulsiveness that draws me back; it's hunger and boredom. Even if it was a need to sit at that table and look out my window, it's okay, Seurat did it too. I realize I am not Seurat, as of yet, but I am just getting started. I am still not sure when siesta starts and stops here, but when I arrived at the bakery it was closed.

My new home, my winter home, is small and lonely but stretches off into the distance. I sat on the wall that buttresses tourists from the drop of the valley and lost myself among the birds. Looming in the background is responsibility. Despite the constitution I create for myself in love letters and on bar stools, I am at heart a stickler. It's a good thing really. Even the details in the most abstract of masterpieces are carefully and precisely laid out, so I'm told. Katie was the same. She wasn't my muse, she didn't bring inspiration, but she did buy me an extra month in Valldemossa.

I received the first letter from my parents this morning. I read it on the wall while waiting for siesta to end. It was news and a list of jobs they thought would be good for me when I eventually came back – drained of money and inspiration. It wasn't phrased like that, it was actually very supportive, but the mention of going *home* wasn't. This is my home, for as long as it lasts and until it isn't.

Later, I was back in my flat faced with my work and all of its possibilities – trying to uncover the correct one. When you come by, I will show you where I am and where I hope to be. I hope you enjoy Valldemossa.

Forever Mine

A. J. Morgan

'I really don't think I can do anything more for you, Jas,' said Dr Metherall.

She paused then looked briefly away. Her right hand rested on her desk, the index finger and thumb pinched together, and she was scratching at a patch of loose varnish. 'I'm sorry, but we've discussed this from every possible angle. I don't wish to sound unsympathetic, but you need to move on. Have you thought about getting away, even for a short break?' She stopped her agitated scratching. 'I might be able to recommend you for some counselling if you think it would help.'

There was an awkward silence. Jasmine said: 'No thank you, Dr Metherall. I don't want to talk to anybody.' She stood up. Dr Metherall's eyes flickered minutely from side to side.

'I'm sorry to have taken up so much of your time,' said Jasmine. 'And yes, I might get away somewhere.' As she closed the door behind her, she heard Dr Metherall open her desk drawer. Jasmine knew she wanted her menthol sweets. She sucked them obsessively between consultations and sometimes, if it was a bad day, in her patients' face.

Callum drove them to Wales in the old Morris Traveller. Fergal lay in the back like a lamb, occasionally getting up stiffly to shift his position, his gnarly claws clacking on the metal floor as he turned before expelling a long sigh and settling back down on his blanket. Jasmine knew he hated the heat – poor old boy. Still, they were over the bridge and it shouldn't be long. Callum had seized upon the idea of going away like a lifeline. She had no idea where they were going. Callum had found it on the internet. By a stroke of luck they had got the house at short notice between bookings. It was somewhere west of Swansea, where he had spent holidays as a child. He whistled through his teeth as he drove and had a jaunty, carefree air.

They turned off at Carmarthen, picked up the keys from the agent and were winding up into the hills. Somehow it seemed hotter than ever now that the sun had started to sink. The landscape lay enervated, sweltering in an amber haze. They had been sent good directions by the owner. After a few miles, they turned off at a lane marked 'New Cross' and there, a few hundred yards on, was the nameplate, the letters beautifully engraved in gold on dark slate. *Ger-y-llyn*.

'How do you pronounce that, do you think?' asked Jasmine.

Callum had a shot at it. 'We used to have a lady who cleaned for us when I was a kid,' he said. 'She taught me a bit of the old lingo. By-the-lake it is, I believe.'

They rounded the line of tall conifers which hid the house from the lane and there was the dark expanse of water, simmering in the declining light. A path of gold glimmered on

71

its surface and swallows dived and skimmed away in the heavy, still air, feasting on the clouds of insects which hung over the water. In the centre of the lake there was a little island where white willow tilted in a ragged mass. Underneath the boughs, a pair of swans opened and closed their wings as they drifted sleepily. Beyond the lake's shores, the house nestled, a long, low white building whose windows and doors had long since shifted cheerily out of alignment.

'How beautiful,' said Jasmine. She sank back in her seat and remained quite still, gazing.

'We ought to get Fergie out,' said Callum. He parked the car in front of the house and hopped round to open the back. Fergal stood on the threshold looking at him imploringly.

'Come on, old chap,' said Callum. He put his arms around the dog's middle and lifted him out gently onto the gravel driveway. Jasmine stood watching with tears in her eyes.

'He's getting old,' she said.

'It happens,' said Callum.

'He's all I've got left of Mummy.'

Callum closed his eyes and massaged them with his fingertips. When he looked at Jasmine again she saw how tired he was. 'It's a natural process, Jas,' he said.

He reached for the bottle of water and Fergal's bowl and let him have a good long drink after the heat of the car. When he had finished, Fergal sat panting and breathing rather heavily.

'It'll be better for him indoors,' said Callum.

It was just as Callum said. When they unlocked the door they were enveloped by a shady coolness. 'These old stone walls come into their own in the summer,' he said. There was a short passageway, then on the left the kitchen and on the right the lounge. It was evident a good deal of money had been spent on the place. The kitchen was fitted with solid oak units, with tiles in a rich, peachy beige with a vine leaf motif running through. Ancient, misshapen beams fused the ceiling.

'According to the blurb, some parts of the house are four hundred years old,' said Callum

Fergal clicked wearily across terracotta flagstones and flopped down, resting his head over his paws.

'I think one of the rooms is made up,' said Callum. 'I'll take the stuff up. A bit mad I guess to rent something with four bedrooms.' He looked at her, suddenly diffident. 'But it is beautiful, isn't it?'

Jasmine smiled at him and said: 'It's lovely. Quite stunning. You go up with the bags. I'll make some tea.'

There was a perfect view from the kitchen. While the kettle boiled, she sat at the enormous oak table, staring out. Little black rags were fluttering over the lake. Not the smooth plunge and rise of the swallows, but a quickened, flickering flight that darted one way and then another, bobbing off the shadows from the trees.

'Are those bats?' she asked when Callum returned.

'Yes, I think so,' he said, resting his hands on the table and peering out.

'I've never seen them before,' she said. She placed her hand on his. 'Thank you for bringing me here.'

He bent down and kissed her. 'Are you feeling any better?' he asked.

'I've still got those pains,' she said.

'Dr Metherall said they're most likely nervous stomach cramps, didn't she, and should pass? Did you change your pill as she suggested?' Not, he thought dryly, that there was much need for the pill at present.

'Yes,' she replied, 'but it hasn't made much difference.'

Then, as though reading his thoughts, she added: 'I'm sorry for everything.'

They drank their tea in silence, listening to the chakking of rooks across the lake.

'I think I'll see if Fergal wants to take a little turn,' said Callum. 'Why don't you have a bath and relax?'

'Yes, I think I will,' she said.

Callum stood up, looked over to where Fergal lay dozing and said: 'Fergie boy? Fancy a pootle?' Fergal staggered friskily to his feet, his head turned on one side and ears pricked. His misty eyes acquired a little gleam.

'He's still game,' said Callum.

Jasmine stood and watched as Callum strolled down to the lake with Fergal waddling at his heels. Occasionally, Callum bent down, put his arms around the old dog's head and kissed him. It touched her acutely to see a man show such tenderness. Callum had always loved Fergal. When her mother had been ill, it was he who had fed him, walked him and given him solace. Fergal loved him in return, more than he ever did her in truth.

She wandered upstairs and found their room. There were casement windows which she threw open to take in the cooling, honeyed air. She undressed, found her dressing gown and slipped it on. In the corridor, she smiled, recalling childhood trips to the seaside in Sussex. Like the crooked house, the floor listed away to one side and had the strangely disorientating effect of pulling you away with it. She found the bathroom, exquisitely done out in beige and burnt orange with deep beige ceramic tiles on the floor, cool on her swollen feet. The sink was inset in gold-flecked granite.

She paused briefly to look at herself in the mirror. Her face had a drained look and her complexion was not good. *I must do something about this*, she thought, *pull myself together*. She

74

started to run the water. Mr Mathias had said he would make sure the water was hot ready for them, and there were bath salts on the rim of the bath. *Mathias – what a wonderful name*, she thought, as she removed her dressing gown. *Biblical and dramatic*. Steam began to rise from the water. She added some lavender salts and stood over the bath, breathing in the heady perfume. She climbed into the water. The heat of it was soothing and the lavender perfume so kind. She closed her eyes. A terrible tension, which had become lodged in her very fibre, began to drain away. She lay back and let the water lap over her. How wonderful to loosen her grip, that fierce and desperate hold on the fabric of her life that had threatened constantly to unravel.

She slid further down into the water. At the back of her mind a voice was saying *don't go to sleep, it can be dangerous*. She tried to open her eyes but they only flickered open and shut again. She did not lose consciousness; her mind simply disengaged from her inert body and quivered, detached.

She could hear her mother crying. 'Come here, Jasmine,' she was saying through her tears. 'Come here and sit on the edge of the bath. I want to look at you.'

Jasmine sat down as she was asked so that she could see herself in the mirror. Round the wooden frame her mother had pinned photographs of Jasmine at two, four, eight years old, with her long black tresses.

'I want you to see, darling, what you've done,' said her mother. 'Now, look,' she said, wiping the last of her tears away. 'Look at your beautiful hair. You're my own princess, but you've spoilt it. How could you have had it cut off? Look how beautiful it was. And your lovely face is too big now, you see. Too big for

75

your elegant frame. Now sit still.'

Her mother turned to the sink, filled with steaming water and hot flannels. 'Sit quite still,' said her mother. 'This is for your own good. It will make your face smaller, slimmer so that you'll be my perfect girl again.' She took a flannel from the sink, wrung it out then struck Jasmine across the face. 'I'm sorry, darling,' she said. 'But you see what you've done and I can't bear it.'

She struck Jasmine again and again, from one side and then the other.

Jasmine sat rigid with shock.

'Mummy,' she said, 'Mummy....'

Jasmine's eyes shot open and she rose up in the bath, gasping. The room was filled with steam. The taps were still running and the bath was almost overflowing. She quickly turned them off, her chest rapidly rising and falling. She was staring wildly, but through the drifting vapour her eyes came to focus on the mirror over the sink. It was drenched in mist except for a round section in the middle which remained watery-clear, like a portal.

There was someone standing in the bathroom doorway. The figure was shadowy and seemed to be wearing something long, like a robe.

'Who's there?' she cried. She staggered up clumsily and clambered out of the bath.

The doorway was empty. Grabbing her robe, she hurried out into the corridor. There was no-one. Further down, on the carpet, she could see darkish patches where wet feet had passed. They entered and left her room. In the bedroom she stood breathing quickly. On the floor by the bedside chair lay a pile of snipped dark curls. She ran to the window. She could see to the bottom of the dusty drive and beyond the conifers a dark figure was moving slowly in the ebbing light, rounding the bend in the lane. She flew down the stairs.

The front door was open and Callum was crouching on the driveway, fondling Fergal's shaggy mane as he ate from his bowl.

'Did you see anyone?' she said, her breath coming in little spurts.

'What?' said Callum. 'Who?'

'There was someone in the house,' she said. 'Watching me. I saw someone in the mirror. And just now, there was someone walking up the lane.'

'Jas,' said Callum quietly, 'I've been here with Fergie for at least five minutes and before that we were walking by the lake. I haven't seen anyone.'

She sank down on the doorstep, shaking. 'There are foot-marks upstairs,' she said. Her arms were resting on her knees and her trembling hands held away from her body. 'And there was some hair. In our room.'

'For God's sake, Jas,' said Callum. 'It was me. I stepped into a marshy patch by the water. My shoes were wet. I went upstairs with Fergie. I wanted to borrow your scissors to cut the fur away from his ears and eyes. It's making him hot.'

'Did you come to the bathroom?' she asked.

'No,' he said, 'I didn't.'

There was a silence. Then Callum said again: 'For God's sake.'

They remained silent as Fergal pushed his bowl about on the gravel, licking up every last morsel.

'I'm going to make some pasta,' said Callum and went indoors.

He had the meal going and a CD on and the phone rang.

'Yes, Mr Mathias,' he was saying as Jasmine came into the

77

kitchen. 'Everything's fine. The house is beautiful. Thanks for making everything so comfortable.' He was silent for a while, listening to Mr Mathias speak. Then he said: 'Thanks Mr Mathias, I'll bear that in mind,' and he laughed as he hung up. 'Some old codger called Brynmor who lives further up the lane,' he said to Jasmine. 'He wanders up and down the road and likes to have a nose at everyone who rents the place.' He looked at Jasmine who sat smiling wanly. 'He's quite harmless, Jas. Just eccentric. That's who you saw in the lane. But nobody came into the house, I promise you.'

They slept that night under a single sheet. The air dripped the scent of honeysuckle. Fergal settled down on his blanket, on the cool kitchen tiles.

Callum woke early and left Jasmine sleeping. He slipped on his jeans and T-shirt, went down and whispered to Fergal to come. The old chap got up with a sprightly totter, sensing a clandestine walk with Callum before the world had quite woken. Callum stepped out in his bare feet and they wandered down to the lake. There was a heavy dew, delicious on his feet. He took Fergal a little way up the lane where it was easier for him to walk.

As they were returning to the drive, Callum saw a figure standing by the gates. A man with his back to them, staring up at the house. He had on a long, dark coat and a cloth cap. As they drew nearer Callum said: 'Brynmor?'

The man turned round with a start. His complexion was purplish, the coat and cap shabby and filthy.

'Bore da,' said Callum and smiled broadly.

Brynmor was looking sideways, shifting from one foot to the other. 'I seen you,' he said, flustered. 'I seen you, up at the house,' and he began to back away.

'Yes,' said Callum, 'we're here for the week. It's okay.'

Brynmor was backing up the lane and saying, 'I seen you.'

'It's all right,' said Callum, but Brynmor turned and shuffled hurriedly away.

'Bore da!' Callum called after him. He was laughing as he turned into the drive.

Walking up to the house, he suddenly realised Fergal wasn't with him. He looked back.

The dog was still by the gates, staring into the line of conifers.

'Fergie!' he called.

Fergal did not move. He seemed mesmerised by something in the trees. *Rabbits*, thought Callum. As he approached, Callum realised the dog was shaking, his eyes fixed and wide, and his breath was laboured in his chest.

'What is it, old boy?' said Callum. As Callum touched Fergal, the dog's mouth opened and his breath escaped in ugly gasps. Still he was staring into the trees and his trembling became more violent.

Callum followed Fergal's gaze. The sunlight fell in a bright glare on the conifers. Callum shaded his eyes. He thought he saw a figure wearing something long and moving in a curious gliding motion between the trees. As his hand touched Fergal's back, the dog fell forward onto his front, his mouth widening and the breath punching into the air in a stricken rasp.

Callum knelt at this side and shouted into the trees. 'Brynmor? Please, if someone's there, can you help me? I need to call a vet – do you have a phone? Please – can you tell me where to ring?'

Fergal slowly sank onto his side, his breath weakening. Callum stared wildly into the trees. A glimpse of that figure moving soundlessly away. He placed Fergie's head in his lap in an

79

attempt to facilitate his breathing. Slowly the heaving of his body quietened to a whisper. When it stopped, a grey pall came into his eyes. Callum's lips were resting against the old dog's face.

'My boy,' he said softly.

When he looked up, Jasmine was running from the house. She was wearing her white nightdress and the light dashed from it in prismatic bursts. She stopped as she reached them, panting.

'He's gone,' said Callum.

In the evening, Callum took Jasmine up some warm milk. She lay quite still.

'The vet rang,' he said. 'She says they use a really professional cremation service near Newport. We can collect Fergie's ashes on our way home.'

Jasmine did not answer at once. Then she said: 'I need to sleep.'

As her mind dizzied into unconsciousness, she was thinking of her mother in her hospital bed. Her hand closed over Jasmine's and she was saying: *I can't bear the idea of your being forty*.

She seemed to wake and could see the room, with light pushing from behind the curtains. But everything had a strangely veiled look as though she were watching though a gauze. A dark figure was kneeling by the bed. She thought: *I have had enough. I don't want any more of this*. She put out her hand, to prove to herself she was alone. It struck the damp skin of someone's face. The robed figure rose and bent over Jasmine, cradling her head in its arms. Its fingers touched her throat. She struggled for breath, but could not move. Coarse linen covered her mouth. *I can't breathe*, she cried, though she knew she had not uttered the words. She was sitting up in her bed, gasping. There was no-one else. She pulled on her nightdress and ran downstairs.

Callum was in the kitchen. He was wearing his ankle-length dressing gown of dark crimson. He was by the window with his back to her, staring out at the lake.

'Callum,' she said.

He turned to her, his face impassive. *What is it now?* his eyes were saying.

'There was someone,' said Jasmine. 'In that room. I think... maybe... it seemed like...'

Callum glanced away with a bitter smile. Then he looked up, straight at her.

'Your mother is dead,' he said. 'You are not the only person to lose a parent.'

'I know that,' cried Jasmine. 'But you don't understand...'

'Oh for Christ's sake, Jas! I understand too well. Your mother was off her fucking trolley.' He was laughing, but savagely. 'That ludicrous palaver of having to call her Veronique when she was Vera Buckfield from Dudley. Christ – I can't believe we all went along with it. Finding out when she was dead she'd knocked years off her age.'

He came close to Jasmine and pushed his face in hers. 'She was a headcase,' he said quietly. 'And she fucked you up.'

'I'm sorry,' Jasmine's voice shook, 'I'm sorry it's been so awful for you. If it weren't for these pains, feeling so unwell all the time...'

'Hah!' Callum spat. 'The illness card.' He stared into her face. 'You're not ill,' he said. 'Not physically, anyway.'

Jasmine sank onto a chair and began to rock slowly but rhythmically. Callum's voice quivered when he said: 'I've had enough. I have to get out of here, this heat....'

He threw off his dressing gown and walked naked out into the white light. He was walking with strange purpose down to

81

the lake. Jasmine ran to the window. The whiteness of his skin, his sinewy form in the pitiless light transfixed her. She saw him wade into the unmoving lake, arch his back then gracefully fall forward into the inky water. At the same moment, she saw the figure standing on the island amongst the straggling willows. Even in the sunlight it had a muted, featureless quality and stood gazing out over the water at Callum's lambent form as it rose and dipped. She was running out of the door and across the gravel, crying out to Callum. She could see him, no longer taking smooth strokes but floundering on the surface of the water.

The figure stood like a shadow in the air, watching. She saw that Callum was struggling to regain the shore but could not. He was trying to pull himself away from something that held him and no sooner had he reached the shallow slopes of lake's rim when he slipped back and the water was lapping around his mouth.

It was as she neared the water that Jasmine saw the figure moving in swift strides though the trees to the edge of the water. 'Callum!' she cried again, and she was wading into the water calling to him, the folds of her nightdress spreading like blossom on the black surface. She reached out for him. His hands went to her neck and clung to her, his weight borne up by her fleshless frame. They threshed in the water, fighting a dark undertow which strove grimly to pull them down. Callum was aware only of Jasmine's body as he held her in the maelstrom before he clambered from the water and fell on the shore.

He lay still while his heaving chest gradually quietened to a slow, even rise and fall.

He sat up. For a long time he remained looking out to the empty, sunbathed island and at Jasmine as she floated languidly like a pale lily on the quiescent water.

Slag Heaps

Diana Beloved

The South Wales of my youth was to me a dreary purgatory of smells and darkened squat buildings, viewed on a yellowing canvas, applied with sooty fingerprints. Numerous power cuts to abate the possible effects of striking miners only worsened this, and it was during one of these that I came into the world, and in a mad fit of drunken glee by my father was named at the Registration for Births and Deaths Office, my names in the same order as Mama's firstborn.

I had been a bouncy child at home with Mama and the others, but I soon had to go to school. On the first day I found the boys abridged my name with affection, and I was pleased and proud at the age of five not to have been persecuted in the way that I had heard others had. It was two or three weeks before I understood that my name, Dominic, already abridged by my family to render it pronounceable, and which had now been abridged to Dom, had meant that all of the boys were calling me, in Welsh, 'Shit'.

A couple of days after this I managed to broach the subject of school with my father.

'I no longer wish to go to school,' I said. 'I will stay at home and help Mama with the baking.'

'Why you feel like that?' he asked with his usual kindly expression.

I grappled with an answer. 'I don't think boys should come to school wearing no shoes,' I said, as the image of a couple of the miners' boys came into my head. I could not reveal my humiliation to him, as he told us he believed he had made the right move in leaving the fertile soils of Bardi, sending back for his wife once he had established his business.

'It is because their parents are poor,' he replied. 'You must pray for them, pray that their Mama and Dad can afford to feed them. You must be kind to them and pray that they soon will have shoes to keep warm and help to protect their feet.'

That night I prayed that the slag heaps which kept the valleys in perpetual gloom, and which served to remind all of us of our various servitudes, would slide down the mountains and flatten all in their wake.

I yearned for the hot sun and the fresh peppers and funghi and Parma ham and the olive groves and coloured gelati, and the mountains peaked with white snow which I would enjoy when we made our next trip to northern Italy to stock up on red wine and other tasty goods. I yearned now to be at a school with children who would pronounce my name and look upon me with love, not with the sneering superiority I had unwittingly enabled. To live somewhere I did not feel angry and hurt.

My upper youth in South Wales was, however, briefly curtailed by the advent of a war, which saw my mother almost forcibly removed from her seaside café and placed six miles inland, she being considered, despite surely having been the inspiration for the cartoonist Giles' 'Grandma', an enemy alien. I found myself transported to a disused prison on the Isle of Man, the floor in the cell I shared with my brother Frank having a lining of pigeon shit which had smoothed and hardened and whitened over the years.

My father fared worse. Imprisoned on a ship to his destination as a With-Out-Papers in America, he and his fellow men were torpedoed by a German submarine, and he spent his last few hours bobbing about in the Irish Sea presumably praying to the God he still believed to be his saviour. Some of his compatriots managed to save their lives, but my moustachioed father was not amongst these. Thus we fellows were at once fatherless, and needed to run the 'business', the café, one of many which had provided early morning coffees for miners over the years. Although when the British Army had first realised their mistake in having my younger brother alongside them as an officer, and my older brother and myself locked up in a prison as enemy aliens, and thus had offered us release to be drafted, we had declined it fairly snootily. Now, at the watery demise of my father, I requested release and this was granted.

So I found myself back in South Wales, in a town overshadowed by the huge conical slag heaps, which came to represent the darkness present in my soul. I knelt and prayed these would spontaneously combust in a marvellous display of pyrotechnics, so that on balmy summer evenings we too would see the breath of a reddening sunset. Or slip, a slithering pile of tailings, slowly down the other side of the mountain. Instead we were left in the shade of the heaps to smell and feel the effluence from the steel works at Port Talbot, which always seemed to blow our way even on balmy breezes.

We carried on, my family, working on the Catholic church so that at least it looked like the house of a benign God; we painted pastel representations of heaven above the altar, and gold scrolling wherever we could find a suitable place (and I can report there were many of these, and the more I found, the more I seemed to find). We imported white marble statues of the Virgin Mary and Jesus himself, and my sisters cleaned and polished the floor after evening mass every Sunday, and picked arms full of flowers daily to place in white marble vases we had imported from Italy, from our region. This white marble was considered to be beautiful but I found it reminded me more of the floor lining in my erstwhile cell than I was happy to admit. Amongst this apparent grandeur and colour I prayed, for hour upon hour, upon sore and bruised knees, for those slag heaps to dissolve in whichever way they saw fit.

'Why you praying so hard and long, Dominico?' asked my mother, when I would return from a very late shift at the pews.

'I am praying for the absolution of sin, the relief of poverty, for the souls of the dead and the unbaptized to be released from their respective waiting places, I am praying for world peace and tolerance,' I would reply, as if my selfish desire to rid the world violently of slag heaps was not sufficiently important.

'You talk to God about so many things!' she said. 'He will hear your prayers.'

Mama wore only black for the rest of her life. She carried on working in the café, selling her cappuccino and gateau, and tea and coffee in brown paper bags, and single untipped Woodbine fags from a jam-jar on the counter, and only retired when Frank and I wanted to start our own gelato business in west London (where the streets were still, allegedly, lined with gold). Once there, we proudly defended ourselves, and our race as Taffies, when in our Saturday fights, we were breaking the noses of the English drunks who insulted us at the pub.

One of my sisters had married a Catholic schoolmaster and they invited Mama to live with them. Mama's retirement was that of a graceful lady, cherished by Maria Luisa Antonia and Don, and their daughter Maria, and in this retirement, and amongst kind Welsh neighbours and friends from the church, with whom she shared her liqueur chocolates and her bottles of red wine imported from Italy, she chased off the image she had had as an enemy, and wicked, alien. She became very, very popular. She was to be found even in her very late years pinning freshly made ravioli to a board to dry whilst the turkey broth was in preparation for lunch for half the town. She warned my wife always to wear a brassiere and a girdle or expect, like she had, to take on a round figure in later years. In her nineties, and watching TV on a Sunday afternoon, she was disappointed to see her grandchildren wanting to watch a cowboy film as she believed that cowboys were dirty and unshaved. She decided to go to her bed for the duration, and was found there lifeless two hours later.

I can only begin to describe, then, how bad I felt, when on the afternoon news back in October '66, the Aberfan disaster, as it has come to be known, was first being announced. I absolutely blamed myself for the whole disaster. Somehow, all that kneeling and praying I had done all those years ago in that little church filled with white marble statues and vases full of flowers, had come to a most unfortunate fruition. Aberfan was in fact a bit of a way from the little town I had lived in, but even so. This must've been my fault.

87

I spoke to Don on the phone that evening as more of the disaster unravelled. He had become the Headmaster of the local Catholic school at that stage, and as such was a town authority, and a bit of a leader in terms of religious understanding. He knew my belief in God had been shaky, if not totally flaky, for a number of years, since, more or less, God had failed to answer those prayers I made on bended knees so many years ago in our church. He told me, almost severely, that I needed to pray to God to know that this disaster was not of my making. That God would forgive me and welcome me back into the fold so long as I would humbly appreciate that I was not ultimately responsible for Aberfan. That the disaster, he believed, had come about through the failure of the National Coal Board to deal appropriately with its by-products. He replaced the receiver rather abruptly, I thought.

I have to say that this was the first time I had to strive to appreciate that God, in whom I did not quite believe anyway, was not Himself responsible for everything and that I, as his human representative on earth, was not therefore the conduit for every passing disaster in the western world. This was epiphanic. It was as though the horrible descent of that slag heap had shifted something so profound in me that I could begin to contemplate my world in glorious technicolour for once.

I have spoken of this to my children but they prefer me to keep to myself the shades of black with which I describe my childhood. For one thing, they have less time for conversational meanderings, all of them having, to some extent, taken on the mantles of professionals, whether as doctors, teachers, lawyers or what-not. They see my conversation as the disappointment and daftness of a sad old man, not as the dexterity of one small

88

person resolving mysteries around God, or the deftness of the same chap tarrying with the human race and its subsection. Then, to be fair, they never saw the curl of an unfiltered woodbine or inhaled raw, sulphurous Port Talbot. I am glad for them that they surround themselves with gay colours. They, to whom God is an oppressive nuisance figure from an earlier age, were born with the lights turned on.

Hospital Green

David Oakwood

Walking those twenty-nine slow steps towards the partially glazed swing doors, Joe recognised the colour on the corridor walls as 'Hospital Green' and allowed his lips to briefly rise in the corners of his mouth. On his return from B&Q just two weeks earlier Nancy had mocked his choice of sample pots for the re-decoration of their inherited bathroom. She had re-labelled the Matt Ochre 'Re-hab Yellow', for its similarity to the stained smoking rooms of psychiatric units, the Chalk Grey 'Empty Swimming Pools' because it made you want to jump into one and the now oppressively familiar 'Hospital Green' was given to the Japanese Jade because all hospitals have walls the colour of diluted snot. Nancy was always right.

As he came to the end of the corridor, the dreaded steps feeling leaden, he took comfort in a memory of Nancy's warm full breasts as she had hugged him before placing her hand on his back, encouraging him forwards towards the arched doors of the hospital's entrance. She'd offered to go with him but he had refused. Since Nancy had never met his father he didn't see the point in her being there. If he'd told her the truth it was that he was concerned she might like him, and he didn't want to have to hold that against her.

He was gushed onto the ward by the stormy swing of the two doors, his hair flushed to his cheeks as a white coat, bleeping and reeking of tobacco smoke, rushed by. He walked the few paces to the nurses' station, where he stood before a cluttered desk, piled with files, papers and Quality Street chocolate wrappers. He was suddenly met by a mouthful of leaning teeth, stacked in a smile between the gold hooped ears of a middle-aged black woman, rearing up from her knees behind the desk. Despite his surprise he still noticed the thickly pasted eye-shadow that rippled out from the pools of two huge brown eyes and wondered what colour Nancy would call this woman's make-up, thinking 'Apricot Binge' as she said 'Can I help you?' in a thick Nigerian accent. Joe paused. Like his slow steps, his reluctance to move forward held his tongue and words hostage.

'Mr Cole. I'm told he's here. Mr Royston Cole.'

She turned away making a clicking noise beneath her tongue and looked at the smeared red ink of a patient list written on the whiteboard behind her. She ran a dangerously long pink finger nail down the names and room numbers, impersonalising his father's care in an instant.

'Next left.'

'Thank you. Is he awake?' That wasn't what he meant; he meant is his face all crooked, will there be dribble running down his chin, will his eyes be lost and glazed?

'See for yourself. Next left.'

91

She looked down then. He was dismissed. He backed away from the desk and took a couple of paces past a wheelchair. Then with great detail he studied a picture hanging in a space cramped by flyers announcing charitable events. The cheap reproduction of Monet's Water Lilies was hung, according to the brass plaque below it, in memory of Mrs Irene White, known as Lily, who had been greatly cared for by doctors and staff on this ward in 1989. Always remembered. The print was faded.

'Next left.'

He looked back to see the nurse shooing him on with the shiny back of her hands. Joe always felt wired in hospitals, his nerves on red-alert, believing, as he had since childhood, that bad news waited under every bed like the crocodiles of his nightmares. He was assaulted by hospitals, the sense of smell under viral attack, through the nostrils and the tongue, where it could be tangible enough to taste. A taste of heated plastic cups holding overly boiled coffee. The taste of fear. Joe was salivating as he turned to approach his father's room.

He'd naively imagined a private room, where they could be re-united away from the prying eyes of other bored or lonely patients. Instead, Joe saw that his father was nursed in a bay with five others and so it was that ten eyes followed him as he walked, his left shoe squeaking, between the rows of metal beds. He was forced to stare into each silent pair of optics, attempting to recognise the Paul Newman blue of his father's. As he searched amongst the faces of these men it seemed that each was cut from the same piece of cloth, and it was a rag so steeped in ill health that it needed wringing out above a sluice of pity. One after the other he sought recognition within the grey lines of facial creasing. And suddenly, finally, there he was.

Asleep. His blue eyes temporarily lost, the approaching

blackness of demise protected from the winking strip lights by his soft puffy lids.

Joe sighed.

He had to check the name above the bed to be certain. His father's hair, brown in his youth, was now a wiry shock of white, crowning him with a lion's mane. He took a seat between the metallic beige bin and the bedside cabinet on which stood a glass vase of conceited daffodils. There was also a card, lying flat on its envelope. Joe didn't dare reach for it in case his father's eyes were to open and catch him prying. He stood up and leant towards it, reading GET WELL SOON DEAR HUSBAND.

His wife was still hopeful.

He looked on his father's prone form. The blue wattle blanket clung to him, the contours showing a wasted body, stones lighter than in health. As Joe sat he found himself picturing the Royston Cole of memory. A powerful man. Huge pumpkin stomach, rock solid to the punch. Biceps you could hang on, tattooed with naked women he made dance through tension and release. Dance! Make them dance. Fits of seven-year-old giggling and a faint smile on a thirty-year-old face.

Joe stared at the sleeping man before him. He watched the chest rise and fall, and noticed in the long nasal hairs of his father's nostrils that a small dried bogey was lifting up and down with the gentle snores. This man had boxed in the army. He'd once been stabbed in a drunken brawl. He'd made cars in factories in the days before machines. Later he'd been a blacksmith, pounding iron into gates and staircases. He'd employed a team of men who'd helped him forge and pay the mortgage. This man was a man's man. A man whose humour was as black as his hands. A lover of motorbikes and engine oil. An archetype. But no longer one of Joe's heroes.

93

Joe's heroes were not hard and sooty. Joe's heroes were men of wit and words, not anvils and hammers. Joe's heroes talked of saving the rainforest not Banger Racing, they marched against war not towards it. Joe's heroes could cry.

He felt weak. A toddler in a lion's cage. He became aware again of the eyes on him and stood and pulled the ugly floral curtains around his father's bed space. He heard an audible 'tut' from one of the other patients, their entertainment over. He sat down. He stood up. He watched his father sleep. What could they say to each other in any case? It had been too long. Who was he here for, his father or himself? They were questions he had verbalised on the journey over. There were no answers then or now. Twenty-three years. A lifetime. Far too much to say and no time in which to say it.

His father stirred a little, shifted his position but did not wake. Joe stepped back, holding his breath, his back pushing open the curtains, allowing a glimpse of nothing to the eager eyes of their audience. He could leave now. He'd been. He'd seen. But he'd not been seen. His frustration flushed his cheeks, or it could have been the close heat of the ward, the smell of an un-emptied bed pan on the other side of the curtains, his thick jacket still worn or the scarf wrapped tightly around his throat. He began to remove the scarf, draped it across the back of the chair, un-buttoned his coat. He couldn't bring himself to remove it. He wasn't staying. He would go. He would go now. He had work to do. Deadlines to meet. An editor to please. He still had a life. His father's was over and he'd not been in it. What right to return now? To stake a claim in this death scene when he'd barely featured in the play. He felt like an extra demanding lines, assuming a right to see his name in the credits. This was over. God damn the phone call and his aunt's warbled pleading words.

'*Please Joe. He doesn't have long. Just for a few minutes. Give him that. He's only been out six months. Please Joe.*'

He sat back down then and reached towards his father's hand. It was huge. Huge thick fingers. Liver spotted now, and pale. No oil or soot. Clean finger nails. A first. His father's hands, once calloused and hardened with graft were soft like putty. They were not his hands. These hands never held him up to reach a football from the clawing hawthorn branches. These hands never nailed a tree house to the willow. These were not those hands that forged the gates through which he rode, his son as pillion passenger clinging, squealing laughter, to his back. These were not those jealous hands that had gripped and squeezed and choked and robbed Joe of his mother.

Royston Cole opened his eyes.

There was no one there.

Gerard's Head

Jamie White

My bed is very important to me. In work, behind my screen, wearing my headphones and microphones and talking to people about their phones, I often (when not pretending that I am the helicopter pilot from *Apocalypse Now*) think about being in bed. For me, bed is warmth, safety, comfort, and occasionally other things. My DVD player is set up at the foot of my bed, and as it is the warmest place in my oppressively cold flat, I seem to spend most of my free time cocooned away from the real outside world, watching 28-inch versions of it.

My life is alarmingly regular, and I have no reason to want to change this. I have all the social contact I need in work, as I am talking to people all through the day. Sometimes a gang of us will go for a few drinks on a Friday or a Saturday. Sometimes we end up going on to a club, or something like that. But not often. Sometimes Dean comes round and we get a pizza and a couple of beers and watch a film. At the moment I don't really want anything else. I feel about entering relationships the way that Orwell felt about writing a new book; that it would be exhausting and doomed to fail. I am, when all is said and done, a normal, twenty-eight-year-old male.

There. I've set the scene for you. Is that okay? I'll get on with the story now, but I'll put it in the past tense. I'm sure I learned the term for this during my degree, but that's long gone now. Ah well.

Tuesday morning. I'd been up until half twelve watching *Once Upon a Time in America*, so I was a little jaded. I hopped out of bed, it is a double since you ask, but it's a long time since I've needed it to be. I had a shower, even though I'd had one the previous night, pulled on a blue shirt and black trousers from Next and went to brush my teeth.

I don't normally make the bed before going to work (or after coming home to be honest), but I leaned down to pull the cover back over when I saw Gerard Depardieu's head.

Not his real head, of course.

On the pillow on the side of the bed that I don't tend to use was a pattern of indentations, creases and folds that were bizarrely reminiscent of the burly Frenchman's face. Well, it looked so cool that I took a photo with my mobile phone, decided not to plump him up and went out of the door, down the stairs and to the bus stop.

On the way I sent Dean a text containing the picture of Gerard's head. He very quickly responded in his usual manner: *Y u send pic of yr bed? U gay or what?* Strange. On my phone Gerard's head was really obvious. You could see his straggly hair, his significant nose, his Gallic grin. I decided there and then not to show anybody else. If Dean couldn't see it, no one else would get it either.

On the way home I rented *Manon des Sources*. After watching it I slept fitfully in a chair to avoid messing up Gerard, but he still managed to infiltrate my dreams, like a member of the resistance delivering razor-blade contaminated pig swill to Gestapo headquarters.

He's a big lad, Gerard. You know, for years I thought he was Gerald, but he's not. He was definitely Gerard not Gerald in my dream. I know, because he introduced himself. It's a bit strange, and at one point there were a few too many dancing penguins in it for my liking, but then they turned into nuns and then Julie Andrews came along, looking like she did in between *The Sound of Music* and *Mary Poppins*, and she started singing, but I'll leave that for now. Gerard, after introducing himself, told me why his head was now sharing my bed.

'Reeshart', he said. 'Reeshart. I 'ave to tell yoo somfing. It is why I am 'ere. I, Gerard Depardieu, 'ave made it. I 'ave fousands of adoring fans. I 'ave a farmouse and a vineyard. I do not 'ave to do anyfing unless it moves me, unless I really want to. Look at youself Reeshart; you are a pawn, a mouse on a wheel. You fink you are 'appy, content. But you 'ave nussing. You are a nobody, and zat is why I, Gerard Depardieu am here. I will make you see zat you are nussing. And zen you will fink about being someone, doing somefing.

'You are a young man, Reeshart, a young man. And yet you live your life like a mere pensioner! You must live and love and drink and dance and sing and love and love, Reeshart. You are a shell of a man becoz you will let no one else into zis bed. Go. Go to work in ze morning and look at the women, just look. Don't speak. Any of zem could be yours. I will speak to you again tomorrow!'

Do you know, he was right. Gerard was making complete sense. My life was drifting away. My job, dull but secure, was making me the same. I had to stop looking at life on DVD disks and get out there and do something about it. But how? The last person to share my bed had lasted two months until she went home to New Zealand with a small part of my CD collection, a bigger slice of my heart and nearly all my self confidence. It was a wonder she had any room in her rucksack for clothes. That was three years ago.

I got out of the chair, went to shave. Stopped. Shaving was something I found dull and tedious. I decided not to. As I left the bedroom *sans* tie, it almost looked as if Gerard was winking at me.

I took Gerard's advice and looked around the office. I hadn't realised before just how many women there were. What's more, the ratio of women to men was like something from *Zulu*, and I was Michael Caine's eye-shadowed officer. I found myself maintaining eye contact for just a little longer than was necessary with several 'co-workers', but followed Gerard's advice and avoided talking to any of them.

On the way home I got out *Germinal*. Bloody hell. Old Zola doesn't half go on. J'accuse you, my friend, of writing long-winded naturalist drivel. Again I slept in the chair. Again I dreamed of Gerard.

'Ha ha, mon ami. You 'ave zem now. You have realised they exist, and now you must know that the looks you are getting today, you 'ave been getting for weeks. Monzs! Alors, tomorrow, you must decide which one you want. It will not be hard. There are women there working wiz yoo, who fink about you every night. What about that little redhead you passed by ze photocopier? Or zat tall girl wiz ze lisp who comes in on a scooter? You know, she has a tattoo just above her buttocks of a little devil. Very notty! And Mary, two desks along. I know, I know. She's married. So what? 'Ave you seen 'er 'usband? A fat brute! Tomorrow. Tomorrow you may speak to zem. Just fink. Fink about wish one yoo want in your bed.'

I didn't ask Gerard how he knew all these things about the girls I worked with. In the dream it just seemed natural. The other thing that felt natural was walking into the office like a predator, like Mel Gibson's cockerel in *Chicken Run*. It felt like I was sweating testosterone, and they were all picking up on it. I asked Alice to get me some photocopying done and got a beautiful smile and a cup of tea, I talked to Jo at the water cooler and walked away with the feeling that she would have stood there all day with me, rather than my usual feeling of gratitude for any female kind enough to spend any time at all with me. Thursday I normally go to the pub for lunch, but today instead of me and Dave eating crisps and playing pool I went with a group of ladies to The Blue Anchor (or The Wanker). I normally steered clear, my steps averted by thoughts of discussions on diets, fashions and babies, but I had a really nice time. I was interesting. At least I felt I was interesting, which surely is the next best thing. And because I felt I was interesting, it felt like everyone else was as well.

Especially Rebecca.

I ended up sitting next to her in the pub. We stayed together walking back to the office and even caught the same bus into town after work. We talked about films and music and how crap it was working in the office. (I hadn't really noticed before. That's a lie. Of course I'd noticed at first, but gradually it just became something that I did.) We said goodbye at the bus station and I walked home past Blockbuster.

The only video left with Gerard in it was *102 Dalmatians*. I thought about avoiding it but realised I had to get it. I've

100

watched worse. I think. Once again curled up on the chair I was visited by Gerard.

'Okay, okay mon brave. It looks like you 'ave made your choice. Tomorrow is Friday. She has nussing planned. Believe me. Nussing. If she says she does, she's bluffing. She weel go out wiz you. Nothing serious. Maybe a few drinks? A meal? Per'aps. But don't seem too keen, eh.'

So that was how on Friday night, rather than a pizza with Dean or a few vertical beers standing round a pillar in my work clothes, I was in an Italian restaurant with Rebecca. How strange. We'd finished the meal by about nine. I offered to pay, but we ended up sharing the bill.

Half-past nine is a curious time, really. Too late to do anything, too early to say goodnight, so I asked her if she wanted to go for another drink.

The drink ended up, as they often do, in the plural and before I knew it we were in my flat with cups of coffee and *Green Card* on the DVD player.

'You know Rich', she said, 'It seems a strange thing to say, but you kind of remind me of Gerard Depardieu. Not so much in looks, more like in the way you carry yourself, the way you are.'

'Really. I'm not sure if that's a compliment or not.'

'Oh it is. Believe me, it is.'

'In that case, thank you very much. Or merci, madame.'

'Especially the way you've been the last week. Unbuttoned shirts, stubble, all that jazz.'

'It was unintentional. I've just been having trouble sleeping and suffered for it in the morning. I'll be spick and span by next week.'

'I think I prefer the slightly ruffled version. Why haven't

you been able to sleep?'

'Really weird dreams, really, really quite strange.'

'Bet I can beat yours.' she said.

'Go on then.'

'For the last week, every night I've been having dreams about Audrey Hepburn. And do you know what she's been telling me?'

'No idea,' I say, grinning like Jack Nicholson.

'That I need to pull myself together, sort myself out, get a nice man. One just like you, in fact.'

The next morning, when I eventually woke up in my bed, I turned to the pillow next to me and realised that during the activities of the previous night, Gerard's Turin Shroud likeness had vanished. There was something much better looking there instead.

Still, he had done his job, and it didn't really matter anyway. I'd been having some really good discussions with Michael Portillo in the tartan of my slippers. And Peter Sutcliffe in my toolbox. With my hammer.

POETRY

One More for the Room:
An Old Father's Tale

Jon Dressel

It is a glad thing, many fathers know,
to make them up, the stories for a daughter
who, well-scrubbed and wide-eyed in her bed,
waits on her regaling into sleep. His plots

veered gothic, there was ever some stock scoundrel,
a Vile Vic or Heinous Henry, out to trick
and rob her of an object she held dear,
and each night, when the dastard's deed was done,

she would, instinctive, clutch her pillow, half
in fear. But not for long; a champion, always,
soon would crash on scene, to send the blackguard
packing, spluttering oaths apace. The Kewpie-doll,

the blanket, the stuffed crocodile, redeemed,
the night light on, she then could safely drowse,
again wrapped in the knowledge of her sure
protection, by Davy Crockett, Stonewall Jackson,

Prince Llewelyn, Sherlock Holmes, the giant
Idris, Owain Glyndwr, and Bill the Moon Man,
high on his great stilts. It was, it seems,
a life ago; now, his daughter years since wed,

mock villains put to bed, he sits some nights
in her old room, surrounded by his cadre
of the once employed. Crockett buffs his long gun,
stalwart Jackson strokes his sword, Idris,

knees drawn, boulders in a corner, Llewelyn
whispers to Glyndwr, Holmes, his loyal pipe lit,
puffs on in the gloom. Bill the Moon Man,
house-tall, peers down from outside. It is

a good scene, he is glad to have them there,
champions to the finish of the storied room
where all things stand at last recovered
as thought sifts slowly towards unhaunted sleep.

The Seeds

Guinevere Clark

She ran her nail
up the seed's seam,
said a few words,
sat it in the soil slot.

The trays lay
in the laundry's sickly steam,
among towers of clothes,
pet bowls.

Each morning the soil lay bare
like there was nothing there.
But she was not unaware,
she could feel
little ruptures,
reaching shoots
tugging away in the dark,
that soundless pulse of creation.

Still it sat flat.
Clothes – damp, hot, mouldy, cold,
got dropped on the trays
like it didn't matter –
this silent mothering.

Then, as the new moon
edged herself out,
they uncurled, like
tiny palm trees,
nine in a circle.

So pure was her joy,
'fresh life', she sighed,
trampling rabbit droppings
back into the baffled house.

That DNA had split
and she had made it,
it was a no bull shit
situation.
Among the tiers and tiers
of red bills,
divorce papers, death...
those seeds had put on
a welcome show,
offered a little lightness,
a reminder that we can re-grow.

Then, she heard his cackle...

The rabbit
had surfed the laundry piles,
from the floor to the top,
now he sat, at home
on the empty square of fresh earth,
an umbrella shoot
at the tip of his smile.

Again, the soil lay bare
and the exhausting husband
crowded in on her,
with a loud and callous grin.
The seeds husks
lay empty and thin
like their love.

The Plates

Guinevere Clark

Snowdrops converge –
vast camps
of tight capsules
laced strong over springs split.

The sea air
shivers,
it has travelled far,
salt sweetens
in pollens beads,
the juicy scent of grass.
Winters edge is falling.

I trudge
under the sun's quickening pulse,
loaded as ever
with the pouches
and scripts of my art –
hanging off me like children.
I've danced all day,
knowing
but not certain of your death.
I'm so hungry now.

I curve the corner
sniffing chips,
track the trail
through puppies, families,
buckets and spades
and there it sits,
like an oasis –
Tenby Chippy.

I enter the fat fog,
the counter's queue,
ask with a strained face to be seated.
It's quiet in the restaurant,
no-one here, but me...

Two plates sit opposite each other,
equally dressed
with the silver skin of scraped out fish.
It is a monument to
a couples feasting.

I tackle my
Alice in Wonderland portion of chips,
soft and oily
and recall the place my Grandparents took me –
a restaurant like this,
so long ago.
They were old then...

The tap of cutlery,
the hum of the fryer,
white tea cups,
screwed in chairs,
foil ashtrays, fizz, straws.

It was a meeting point,
for the family,
halfway
and we'd all have fish and chips,
in the middle.

I nearly knew my Grandad had gone,
as I wound through Wales on the bus
this morning.

What a day he'd chosen,
with the first hot bolt of spring
stirring the nation
from its icy sleep.

Now,
seated at my halfway point,
between here and there,
knowing and not,
the twin plates
squared close up to my Grandparents' ghosts
and they were happy and nourished,
present yet gone,
side by side like their beds.

I sat in the melted shop
for as long as I needed to,
among heaven's fresh rays,
the simmering fish.

As I left for my bus,
the waitress glided
like a nurse
to the pair of plates,
I didn't stay to see her take them.

Daisy in the Snow

Jamie White

Last night it snowed
And after forty-eight congratulatory psychic birthday calls
And six hundred and eighty-five messy breakfasts
We skid out of bed, you and I.

Snow is cool, you say, stuck like a sparrow to the window.

We post a snowman on our front step
And then
Your doughnut hand in mine
We swing and slide to the park, hunchbacked in white.

And before you were and I was barely
I climbed a mountain made of snow
(The top at least)
A picture of me toast faced and tearful
Sleeps in a box you haven't seen
With smilers who never met you.
Chilled by frail ice, warmed by exertion.
My lavender breath floating
On the earth's constant curve.
Now ten years melt like lava runs
And my glacier climb is a stubbly scree.

The coin-eyed snowman already puddles his way to the sea
And I, expecting liquid salt to melt our doorstep trap
Lift a Stalingrad carrot from the floor.
Turn to see you waltzing,
Your boot heel on his slushy corpse

I wonder, when the dawn cries on my frosty form
If it will draw from you a wilder yelp
As I melt into the leaf-filled gutter of your memory.

dog on a rainy street

Tinashe Mushakavanhu

i am an exile in wales, the black apparition
darting along the one-way king street in carmarthen

my past lies far   far behind me
it is this diaspora route i have taken, but no
it has bilingual signposts that do not speak my language
nothing points back
          where i came from

life is not a straightforward highway with signposts giving
directions
          warning: it has NO EXIT

life is a black stray dog searching for shelter in this rain and cold
          it is me

Barbie Girl

David Oakwood

At nine

they drank orange squash

ate jelly

and she had nine pink candles

on her Barbie cake.

In bed

she rubbed Ken's blunt cod-piece

up

and

down

Barbie's smooth numb knickers.

At eighteen

she drank orange squash vodka

ate ecstasy

and had one red candle

in her Sainsbury's muffin.

In bed

she rubber Johnny-ed men

in

and

out

her cheap nylon knickers.

At nineteen

his cod-piece throbbed

like her throat

beneath fist-tight fingers.

When they found her

she was as

numb as Barbie's knickers.

Leo
(My lovely son who died aged six)

Naomi K. Bagel

Please be gentle on his first night there,
Please remember the way I used to brush his hair.
Please...
There isn't much to say,
On his first night there,
Do things my way.

Sonnet for a Footballing Man

A. J. Morgan

My father was a footballer, a pro,
But I – to spite him? – never kicked a ball.
Too young, too glib, too self-absorbed to know
How his loss would precipitate the fall.
A young man's glory on the field is sweet,
Adulation the heart's sly narcotic;
Time's whistle-call impossible defeat
And the rush of alcohol a winning kick.
A weapon of articulation made;
His lame defence a self-imposed exile
In the hinterland of a loveless shade
Touched on occasion by a lofty smile.
 Tongueless, limbless – freed by death's consigning;
 I am condemned to seek his soul's defining.

Cynddylan, sahib

Davena G. Hooson

The red light stops me by woodland.

The parched ditch spawns spiralling dervishes of dust.
The steady hum of insects harmonise in eastern intervals.
A blackbird sings over grasshopper saranghi.
Garlands, cream and white, froth along the roadside,
straining after passing cars
like acolytes.

Slowly,
Tractor approaches.

In its glass howdah the bouncing occupant,
be-capped, his waist tied tight with baler-twine,
makes his progress.
Reaching beech twigs stroke the handle,
brush the dust off,
make namaste.

The traffic light stands alert, its cap of office arresting the sun.
A parsee bumble bee, veers through mazes of hot air.

At the light's green signal I move on.

Mirror image –
the tractor is a mirage,
leaving, in Llanddewi, the pungent air-print
of India.

Tell Us Something About Yourself

Menna Elfyn

At twelve, my table was laden with silence;
I had nothing to say to anyone,
no passing squalls of chit-chat,
no curds-and-whey cloudy tall tales,
no lightning-strike of story.
I was silent, sucked into my flesh.

'Tell us something about yourself,' said Father,
above our daily bread;
and I would, hesitantly, reach for a morsel,
holding my fork high so I wouldn't drop it.
easier, though
to carve the roast with a whetted knife
than break the bread of conversation;
more painful to pass the time chatting
than pass a hot dish, sorting the peas and queues.

Language was a fast for one.

The phrase comes back to me now:
the impromptu 'tell us about yourself'
above the delegates' banquet.
I never ever believed
I'd spend my life filleting words.

I am contented to be mute,
sat at a board weighed down
with no judgement but excess:
and yet, I am greedy for crumbs
that are no more, when you shake life's cloth
than words on the cold, hard breath of the wind.

Translated from the Welsh
by Elin ap Hywel

Contributors Notes

Naomi Karon Bagel is a dyslexic who left school at twelve years old and has now graduated with a BA at Trinity College, where she is also an MA student in Creative Writing. A performance poet, she has had work published in *Cambrensis*, *Red Ink*, *Roundyhouse* and other community magazines.

Diana Beloved is a poet and artist.

Guinevere Clark is a belly dancer and poet from Pembrokeshire. Her poetry collection, *Fresh Fruit and Screams*, has been reviewed as; 'vivid, dramatic, sometimes unsettling, maybe even downright disturbing, but whatever you wish to call it, it is extremely well written'. See www.freshfruitandscreams.co.uk

Jon Dressel is an American poet and creative writing teacher. He runs a bar in St Louis, USA.

Menna Elfyn is a leading Welsh poet with numerous publications in both English and Welsh. She is Writing Director at Trinity College, Carmarthen.

Tyler Guthrie was born in Seattle, Washington. He studied writing and media at Trinity Western University in British Columbia. Tyler tends to draw inspiration from mythology and history.

Megan Haggerty grew up in the small town of Copperopolis, California. She received her Bachelor's Degree in Cinema and Television Arts: Screen writing at California State University, Northridge in 2004.

Davena Hooson is from Carmarthen. She has lived in the West Indies and Northern England but in 1976 returned to Wales. A retired primary school teacher, Davena was inspired to write by her husband and daughter, who are both poets.

Mary Houseman has an MA in Local History from Trinity College and is studying for a BA in Archaeology at Lampeter University. Her teenage novel, *Bluestones*, was published under the name Mary John, winning the Tir-na-nog Award in 1983. She has recently published *The Llawhaden Book*, a history of her parish.

Liz Hambley retired on health grounds from British Airways and lives with her husband, grandson and specially-trained personal assistance dog. She decided to develop her long standing interest in writing by enrolling on the MA course at Trinity College, Carmarthen.

A. J. Morgan was born and brought up in Essex of Welsh and East End parentage. He trained and worked as an actor and now lives just outside Carmarthen where he runs his own business. His passion for writing stretches back to early teenage years.

Tinashe Mushakavanhu is a young Zimbabwean writer. He received a First Class honours degree in English Literature from Midlands State University. He has published several short stories and poems in various anthologies and magazines. He is completing work on his book, *The Harare Hermit*.

David Oakwood graduated in English and Anthropology and trained as an English teacher. He is writing his first novel, a poetry collection and a series of stories for children. Originally from Oxfordshire, he lives below the Preseli Mountains with his wife Sarah and their children, Elsie, Flora, Wilfred and Hazel.

Jamie White has worked as a food writer, stand up comic and session musician but is now just a teacher. He lives in Swansea with his wife and two kids.

Acknowledgements

The editors and contributors would like to thank Trinity College, Carmarthen for its support and funding of this anthology and in particular MA Creative Writing Course Directors Dr Paul Wright and Menna Elfyn for their guidance and encouragement and Kevin Matherick, Head of Faculty of Arts and Social Sciences, for his support. We would also like to thank Dominic Williams and Lucy Llewellyn at Parthian Books whose advice on the preparation of this volume has been invaluable, and also Peter Florence, Director of the Hay Festival, and Bob Mole, Schemes Officer at Academi, for their expert assistance in the promotion of the book.

A special thanks to the *A Haunting Touch* committee:
Editors: A. J. Morgan and Tinashe Mushakavanhu
Cover: Tyler Guthrie, David Oakwood, Guinevere Clark
Marketing/Promotion: Davena Hooson and Megan Haggerty.

PARTHIAN

parthianbooks.co.uk

diverse probing

profound urban

epic comic

rural savage

new writing

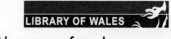

Independent
Presses
Management

INPRESS

inpressbooks.co.uk

gwales.com
Llyfrau ar-lein
Books on-line

PARTHIAN new writing

parthianbooks.co.uk